# TARGET OF VENGEANCE

## A NOVEL OF SUSPENSE

### REBECKA VIGUS

OPEN WINDOW

Livonia, Michigan

# TARGET OF VENGEANCE



Published by Open Window
an imprint of BHC Press

Library of Congress Control Number:
2017951269

ISBN: 978-1-946848-82-6

Visit the publisher at:
www.bhcpresss.com

# ALSO BY REBECKA VIGUS

Macy McVannel Novels
*Rivers Edge*
*Crossing the Line*
*Sanctuary*

Other Novels
*Out of the Flames*
*Secrets*
*Rescue Mountain*

Non-Fiction
*So You Think You Want to be a Mommy?*

Poetry
*Only a Start and Beyond*

Children's Books
*Of Moonbeams and Fairies*

Multi-Author Collections
*In Creeps the Night*

For my daughter, Jamie, who has heard
my stories all her life and never complained.

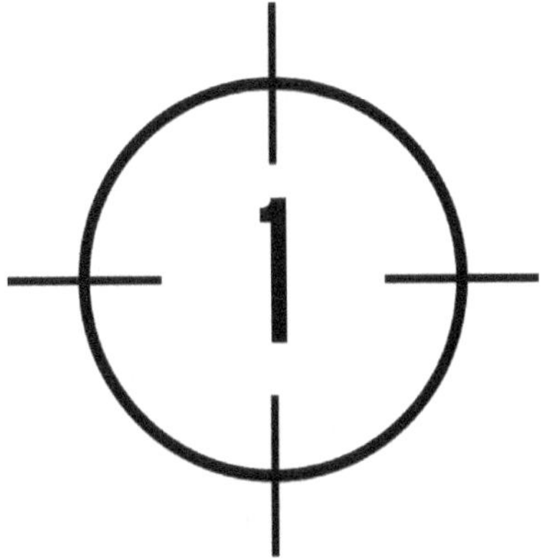

Maggie Parsons smiled as she walked down the hall. Her chestnut hair was pulled up into a bun on top of her head and the beige linen suit she wore outlined her lithe figure. The only sound was the echo of her heels tapping the floor. She had waited a long time to become a principal. Her first job took her back to her own elementary school. How small it seemed now. It had seemed so large to her when she was a child.

The center of the building was two stories high. It had a wing off either end. The offices had been moved to the south end of the building so people entering the main doors would enter in the office area. With the way things were today, you wanted to be sure you knew who was in your building at all times. The best way to do it was to have people sign in at the main office, and of course lock all the other doors during the school day.

Maggie hated the fact the children had to be locked in to be safe. Schools should just be safe. Parents should never have to worry about their children when they were at school. Times, like everything else in life, change and the world today made schools targets.

In another week the children would be crowding the halls. Pre-school, kindergarten, and first grade were in the south wing. Second grade was on the first floor of the central building and third was on the second. The north wing housed fourth and fifth grades. It was a nice set up. Maggie liked it.

It was almost time for her to go home. She took her last walk around the halls. She remembered what it was like when she was a child and smiled. As she was coming down to the first floor, she heard deep male voices. She quickly slipped off her shoes and picked them up. She made her way closer to the stairwell to see if she could determine who was in the building. Her secretary had gone home thirty minutes ago and the night custodian was not due in today. The building should be empty. She wondered who these men were.

"I thought I heard her walking this way," said an unseen man.

"Well, you thought wrong. She's not here," was the gruff reply.

"Her car's still in the parking lot."

"You can search upstairs; she was probably leaving when you heard her."

"Ok, where are you going?"

"To take care of business, I want this building to be unusable before the sun comes up tomorrow."

Maggie quickly slipped into the restroom and pulled out her cell phone. She dialed 9-1-1 and whispered what was going on. She hung up quickly and hid in a stall. She pulled her feet up so the stall appeared empty. She could hear heavy footsteps then she heard someone trying each of the classroom doors. The footsteps were coming into the restroom and closer to where she hid. Her heart pounded and she wished for some sort of weapon to defend herself. All she had was her shoes.

It was then she heard the sirens, as the police roared up in front of the building. Maggie heard the heavy footsteps scurrying away. She expelled the breath she had been holding and waited a few more minutes, then stepped out of the stall and put on her shoes. As she reached the top of the stairs, an officer was coming up. He glanced up and saw her.

"Mrs. Parsons?"

Maggie nodded her head not trusting her voice.

"I'm Officer Evans. I thought our dispatcher told you to stay put," he scolded.

"I'm sorry. When I heard you pull in, I also heard one man walk away. I waited a few minutes," she replied sheepishly. "I just came out."

"Well, come on down. I have a couple more men searching every room. We want to make sure this place is locked down when you leave." He took her arm as she came down the stairs and made sure she got to the ground floor. Together they walked to her office to wait for the other officers to finish checking out the building.

When they reached the office, Officer Evans motioned Maggie to a chair. She sank into it gratefully, not yet trusting herself to stay standing.

"Tell me what it was you heard, Mrs. Parsons."

"I was making a last walk through of the building and heard two very deep male voices. Since the building should have been empty I was suspicious. I took off my shoes and tried to get closer to them so I could hear what they were saying."

Officer Evans looked at Maggie's pale face and prompted, "What did they say?"

"One said something about not being able to find me and my car had been out in front, the other said something about wanting the building to be unusable by tomorrow."

"Do you know what he meant by unusable?"

"I have no idea. Why would someone want to make the school unusable?" Maggie asked. "Why did they want to find me? Have there been problems here?"

"I'm not aware of any, here comes Officer Smith, maybe he found something?"

"Didn't find anything or anyone," said Officer Smith as he came into the office. "I sent Brown out to go around the outside of the building, and check all the doors and windows."

"Good, now let's get this place locked up and see Mrs. Parsons to her car," stated Officer Evans.

"Thank you, both," Maggie said, "I feel so foolish."

"Nonsense, we want you to feel safe at all times," Evans replied.

The three of them locked the doors and walked to the parking lot. Officer Brown joined them there. "Nothing seemed out of place and no one suspicious was outside. All windows and doors are closed and locked."

"What a relief," Maggie said breathlessly, "but where could they have gone?"

"Good question, I think we'll get you in your car and on your way, then walk the outside of the building again and keep a car patrolling by here all night."

The officers made sure Maggie was in her car. She thanked them again and headed home.

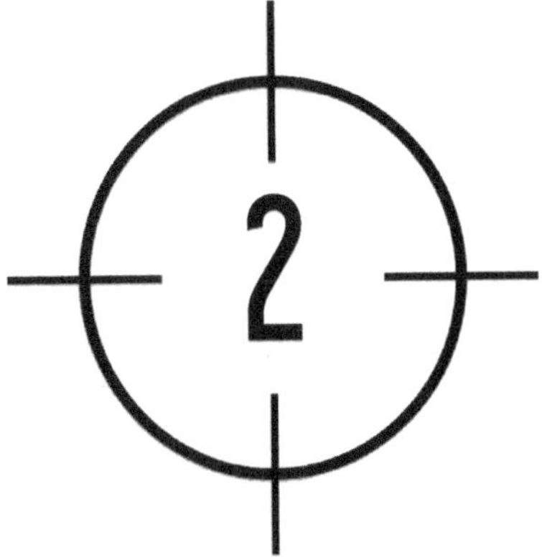

As Maggie drove home she thought about what had just happened. She knew they had been looking for her and wondered why. She wondered what kind of business the one was taking care of and where on earth they had disappeared to when the police showed up. What had the man meant when he said he wanted the school unusable? Why would he want it unusable? It was very puzzling to her. This was not the way she remembered Timberview.

Timberview was a village nestled in the woods. Logging was the biggest industry in the area. The lumber mill had employed those who had not worked in the woods. The houses were neat little ranches. None of them stood out. Most were white clapboard. A couple had been aluminum sided and one or two were painted a cream color. Each had a small porch on the front. It seemed like everyone gathered on their porches on Sunday after the noon meal.

Kids played in the yards. They climbed trees and rode bikes. The field across from the school had been where they went to play baseball. Since everyone knew everyone, no one worried about the kids. The kids knew they had to behave because anything they did wrong got back to their parents before they got home. People just watched out for each other.

Maggie had been away since she was eighteen. She'd gone to college and earned a degree in teaching. She'd moved to start her career. It had been shortly after she started teaching she married, Ben. He'd been the love of her life. He was tall with dark wavy hair and piercing blue eyes. They had been more than friends, they'd been soul mates. They'd started a family and things had been wonderful. Now, she was back at home. Her mother told her about the principal opening right after the accident. She'd wanted a change of scenery. She thought it would ease the pain. Twenty years had not brought much change to Timberview, at least not on the surface.

Maggie was glad to see her mother's house. She took a deep breath before she entered. She was not ready to share this with her mother, who was already worried about Maggie's mental state. She had not been ready for Maggie's nightmares. Maggie was wondering how long her mother would be able to handle them and if she should look for a place of her own.

Turning into the driveway, Maggie just looked at the little house. It was cream sided with a pale blue trim. It looked welcoming with flower beds lining the sidewalk. Heaving a big sigh, Maggie drove in and parked. She took a deep breath and headed for the back door.

Her mother was in the kitchen. Smells from the stove made Maggie's stomach growl.

"Hi, Mom! I'm home," she called.

"Of course, you are, dear," her mother replied. "Why don't you come into the kitchen and tell me about your day? I've put the water on for tea."

"I'll be right there." Maggie didn't wonder how her mom knew about her day, but she did know she would have to fill in the details. She took another deep breath and headed toward the kitchen.

Estelle Mills was small in stature, which didn't make her any less formidable. She could pry information out of a person in a coma, Maggie was sure of it. She'd never been able to hide things from her mother when she was a child, why should it be any different now. She looked at her mother, stirring a pot on the stove. Estelle was wearing blue jeans and a peach colored top with an apron covering them. Her snow white hair was pulled up in a fashionable French twist. She'd put on a few extra pounds, but laughed at her weight saying, "Grandmothers can't be skinny."

Maggie moved into the kitchen and sat down at the counter. Her mother poured the tea.

"So, why did the new principal at Timberview Elementary need to call the police today?" she asked calmly.

"There were a couple of intruders in the building," Maggie replied.

"Did the police catch them?"

"No, Mom," Maggie said sadly.

"Well, I hope they are still looking," her mother said indignantly.

"I doubt it. They probably think I'm some kind of flake."

"I cannot imagine why they would think so," Estelle said. "What aren't you telling me, Margaret Ellen?"

Maggie shook her head, "Nothing, Mom. I just felt frustrated because I'd heard these two men and there was no trace of them when the police arrived." Maggie could see no point in telling her mother how frightened she'd been when one of the men was looking for her.

Her mom patted her hand and said, "I'm sure they will be on the look out."

"You are probably right," Maggie replied. "I'm going to change, and then I'll set the table."

"Fine, dear."

Maggie took her cup of tea with her and walked toward the bedrooms. Funny she thought I have to go through the living room to get to the bedrooms. This seems an odd way to set up a house.

Her own house had an upstairs. The kitchen led to the dining room and from there you could go into the living room. The stairs had gone up out of the formal entryway.

Although walking through the living room to reach the bedrooms seemed odd to Maggie, the familiarity brought comfort.

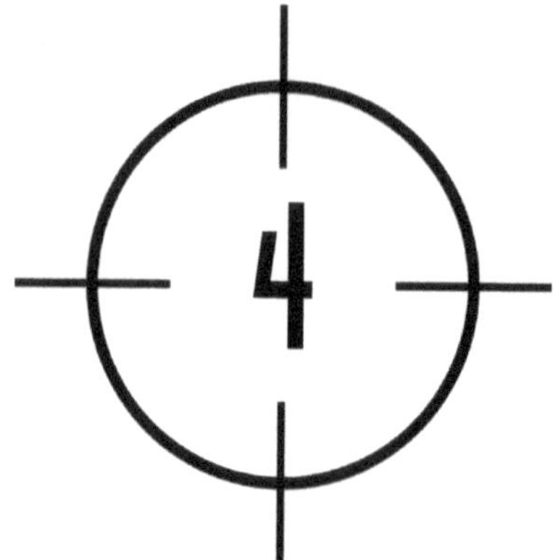

The call came at about 2 a.m. It startled Maggie out of a deep sleep. Her mother came in quickly to see what was going on.

"Mrs. Parsons, this is Sheriff Norton. There has been an incident at the school. We're sending someone to pick you up."

"I'll be ready in five minutes," she responded.

"Okay, I have an officer on the way."

She hung up the phone and looked at her mother. "There's been some kind of incident at the school. I have to go."

"Not without me you don't." Estelle turned and headed toward her own room.

Maggie quickly dressed in jeans and a t-shirt and went into the living room. Her mother was there a minute later.

"Did the Sheriff say what kind of incident?" she asked.

"No, but if the Sheriff is there, it must have been major."

The lights of the police car reached them first. Both women went out onto the porch.

"Mrs. Parsons?" asked the young officer as he looked at both women.

"I'm Maggie Parsons."

"The Sheriff wants me to bring you right away," he said anxiously.

Maggie started down the stairs toward the waiting car; her mother was right behind her.

"I'm coming, too."

"I guess it will be all right," the young man said reluctantly.

Maggie got into the passenger seat while her mother took a seat in the back. When the officer got in she asked, "Can you tell me what happened?"

"It'd be better if the Sheriff told you, ma'm."

Maggie nodded and watched as the small town flew by. The flashing lights from the car were mesmerizing.

In the back seat Estelle had a thousand questions, but kept her mouth closed. She was worried about Maggie and what this might mean. How could something go wrong?

There were police cars, fire trucks, and an ambulance in front of the school when they pulled up. Maggie could see there was also a crowd of people gathered. She was sure it was people from right around the school.

The Sheriff approached the car. "Mrs. Parsons, it seems you were right this afternoon. Someone was up to mischief at the school. One of my officers decided to make an extra pass by the school. It's a good thing he did. He caught a man coming out of the building with a gas can."

"Oh, my goodness!" Maggie exclaimed. "Why was he trying to destroy the school? Who was this man? Will the building be safe for the children next week?"

"Slow down, Mrs. Parsons, slow down," the Sheriff replied. "Let me answer one question at a time. First, we are not sure exactly what he was trying to do. Second, the man is Austin Howard, and third, the building will be fine with some clean up."

"Austin Howard?" Estelle said incredulously.

"Yes, Mrs. Mills," said the Sheriff.

"What on earth was *that* simpleton thinking trying to ruin, my Maggie's school?" she said indignantly.

"Mom, it's not my school," Maggie said quietly. "It belongs to the people of Timberview. They have just hired me to work here."

"Nonsense!" her mother said sternly. "As the principal it IS your school."

Maggie new better than to argue with her mother when she was like this, so she turned to the Sheriff and said, "What can I do to help?"

"Take a walk through the building with me, and then we can get it locked up for tonight. I'll post a car here."

Maggie agreed to walk through the building with the Sheriff.

"What might Mr. Howard have against you?" he asked as they checked the class and supply room doors.

"I cannot imagine he has anything against me," Maggie replied, "Why do you ask?"

"Just trying to get the whole picture," said the Sheriff as they finished. "In the morning, you can assess the damage and get a custodial crew in here working. Otherwise, just go home and get some sleep now. I suspect Mr. Whitehead will want to speak to you in the morning."

"Thank you, Sheriff. I'm sure he will. Can someone take my mother and me back home? I'd like to get some sleep before morning so, I will be ready to face the tasks at hand."

"Of course, I'll send the officer who brought you here to take you home." So saying, he walked away calling for the young officer to drive the ladies home.

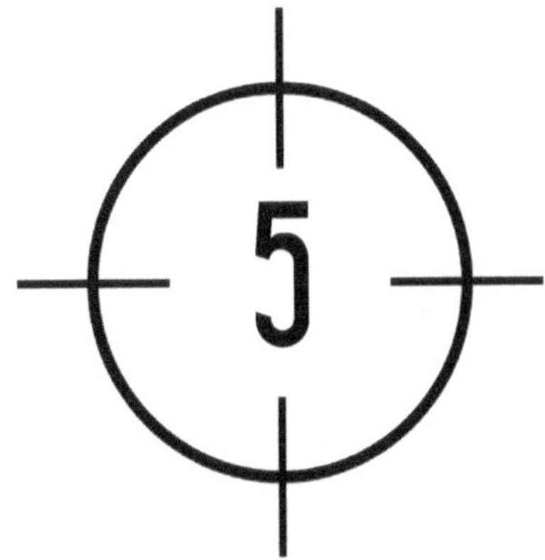

E stelle was very quiet on the ride back. Maggie wondered what her mother was thinking. To make the drive less tense she began talking to the officer.

"The Sheriff told me a man had been arrested," she said softly.

"Correct. Crazy fool was coming out the front door like he owned the place," the young man said. "You just can't predict what the criminal mind will do."

"Is Mr. Howard a criminal?"

"I'd say so after this stunt. But if you're asking was he before, not to my recollection," he replied.

"Does Mr. Howard work near the school?"

"He was fired from the school last spring."

"Oh," she said, "do you know why?"

"I can't recall, but if it would help any I'll tell the Sheriff you were asking."

"Thank you. It helps to have all the facts before rushing to judgment."

"You're right, Ma'm," he said politely.

In the back seat, Estelle listened to her daughter ask questions. She wondered what Maggie was trying to find out. Austin Howard had great potential as a young man. He'd married beneath himself and it had brought him down. Maggie hadn't been there to see it.

They quickly returned to the Mills home. Both women thanked the officer and went into the house.

"Maggie, do you want a cup of coffee or tea?"

"No, thanks, Mom, I just want to get back to bed," she said as she headed for the bedroom.

"Are you sure you don't want to talk about this?" Estelle prodded.

"Yes, Mom, we will talk about it at breakfast. Right now it is three o'clock in the morning and I am tired." Maggie entered the bedroom and closed the door. She had a good idea what her mom wanted to discuss and she did not want to talk about Austin Howard in the middle of the night. This was not high school. She quickly slipped into her pajamas and crawled into bed.

In the kitchen, Estelle brewed a small pot of coffee. Maggie was not going to brush this under the rug. She would find a way to make her talk about Austin Howard. Was this business at the school tied to Maggie's high school days? Or was this because Austin had been discharged last spring? Estelle would get to the bottom of it one way or another, even if it meant making Maggie angry. She finished her coffee and went to bed.

M aggie rose early the next morning. She quickly dressed and went for a run. This had been her morning routine for so long she automatically did it. When she returned, her mother was in the kitchen making breakfast.

"Maggie, you really shouldn't go out so early. It isn't proper, for the new elementary principal to be seen running all over town before decent people have had their breakfast," her mother scolded.

"Mom, I've been running every morning for years. I will continue to do so for many years to come. Maybe you will want to join me one day," she replied hopefully. When she got no response she added, "I'm going to shower then I'll be ready for breakfast."

Her mother sighed. 'Where did I go wrong?' she wondered. It seemed like she and Maggie were at cross hairs most of the time. At least she hadn't had one of those dreadful nightmares last night. Those set Estelle's teeth on edge. Maggie screaming at the top of her lungs in the middle of the night, it was awful. If it kept up, she was sure the neighbors would start talking. No, they had to get some things settled very soon.

Maggie returned to the kitchen dressed in dove grey slacks, a pale pink, tailored, short sleeved blouse and carrying a jacket matching her pants. Her hair was again pulled up and twisted into a bun.

"Where are you off to this morning?" her mother asked.

"I will need to go to the school, assess the damages, make sure the custodial crew is there, and speak with Mr. Whitehead," Maggie responded. "Then I will most likely have to talk to Sheriff Norton."

"I see," Estelle said, "and what about talking to me?"

"Mom, what do you mean? We talk everyday."

"I mean," Estelle said pointedly, "we need to talk about Austin Howard, the nightmares you keep having, and the accident."

"Mom, I'm starting a new job. The nightmares are nothing and will go away," Maggie said with a frustrated sigh. "As far as the accident, I am doing okay with it, I don't need to talk about it."

"Well, I do!" her mother said vehemently.

Startled Maggie looked up from her breakfast and stared at her mother. She had not thought much about how her mom felt about losing a son-in-law and grandchildren. She had been too wrapped up in her own grief to even care.

"I'm sorry, Mom," she said quietly. "Maybe we can take a drive later and talk."

"I'd like to very much," Estelle replied stiffly. "In the meantime, do you think Austin was trying to get back at you?"

"What on earth for?" Maggie asked incredulously. "I've only been in town for about three weeks. I haven't even seen him."

"Well, you kids weren't very kind to him in high school."

"Mom, it was twenty years ago. I can't imagine he held a grudge."

"Some people do."

"In any case, Aussie brought it all on himself," Maggie said defensively. "Imagine trying to make everyone believe he was Australian."

"He was just a kid and new to the town," her mother said reproachfully.

"He had the looks, just not the personality," Maggie reflected. "All the girls were crazy about him until they got to know him better."

"I remember the first time he came here," Estelle said, "He was such a polite young man. Why, he even brought me flowers."

"Yes, he was polite at first," Maggie reflected, "His fake Australian accent had us all drooling over him. We'd never met anyone who lived in a foreign country."

"I remember he was all you talked about for months," Estelle said.

"Yes, we all talked about him," she said. "Then there was the horrible day when his father showed up during baseball practice. He was drunk and abusive, but he wasn't Australian."

"You kids never let him live it down. You excluded him from everything. Did it ever occur to any of you being Australian helped him to escape his home life?"

"Mom, we were just kids," Maggie defended, "all we knew was we had been duped. We were not about to let him get away with it."

"Revenge," she said disgustedly, "you should have just let it go, all of you."

"Well, Mom," Maggie replied, "it's in the past now. When I look back I can see how we hurt him. I'm sure it's been forgotten."

"We'll see," Estelle said not believing it. "We'll see."

They ate the rest of the meal in silence. Maggie put her dishes in the sink, put on her jacket, picked up her purse and keys, and headed for the back door. She turned back to her mom and said, "I didn't know how you felt about Aussie. I'm glad you shared."

Her mother just stared as she watched her daughter leave. 'How could she not have known,' Estelle wondered. 'I tried for two years to get her to take his calls.' She shrugged her shoulders and began doing the breakfast dishes. She would meet with the ladies auxiliary this afternoon, and they would have all the latest gossip. There would be speculation as to why Austin Howard was dumping gasoline inside the school. Some of the speculation would even include Maggie she was sure.

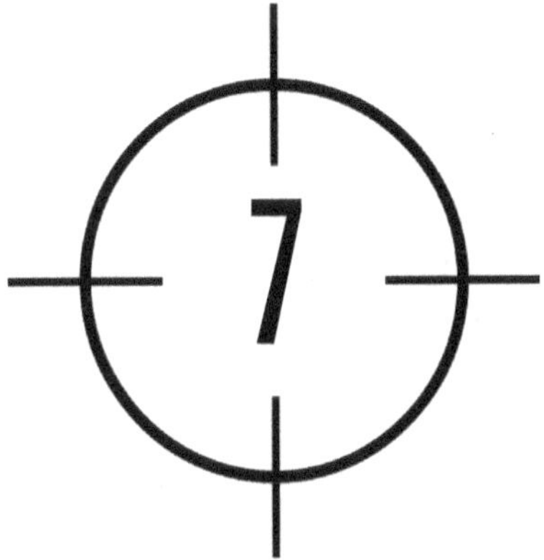

Maggie drove quickly to the school. There she found the custodial staff busy cleaning up the mess made last night. Luckily none of the classrooms had damage; it was all confined to hallways and stairwells. Bob Addison assured her they would have everything ready to go by Monday morning and she should stop worrying. She then went to her office to call Mr. Whitehead.

His secretary said he'd be right with her. "Good morning, Maggie, what do you know about last night?" he asked.

"I know they arrested Austin Howard, and our custodial staff will be finished cleaning the mess by tomorrow. We will be ready for kids in another week. Damage was limited to the halls and stairwells," she replied frankly.

"Good, glad you are on top of things," Mr. Whitehead responded. "What do you know about Austin Howard?"

"Very little at this time," she replied, "he attended high school here the same time I did. I understand he was fired from his job with the school last spring."

"Well, yes," Mr. Whitehead hesitated then continued, "he was in our maintenance department. It seems he frequently showed up late for work and inebriated."

"I see," Maggie said thoughtfully, "Would he have any reason for targeting this building?"

"The only connection he has to the building would be you."

"Didn't he do maintenance here?" she asked.

"No, he was assigned to the middle school crew."

"Ok, thank you," she said. "I will be going over to speak to the Sheriff in a few minutes. Would you like me to report back to you?"

"It won't be necessary," he said. "Sheriff Norton will keep me up to speed on things. When you are done there just enjoy the weekend."

"Thank you," she answered. Maggie wondered what on earth she had stepped into. How could this be her fault? She hadn't seen or spoken to Austin Howard in almost twenty years. She would have to think on it, meanwhile she was heading to the Sheriff's office to see what she could learn there.

Across town at the Sheriff's office, Terry Norton was having his third cup of coffee. He raked his hand through his tousled blond hair. His blue eyes had dark circles under them indicating fatigue. He hadn't had much sleep. They'd questioned Austin Howard most of the night. He'd grabbed a few zees on the sofa in his office. He looked at his rumpled uniform and shrugged. Maggie Parsons had called and she was on her way over. There wasn't much he could tell her, but there was a lot he wanted to ask. He'd start with why she decided to come back to Timberview.

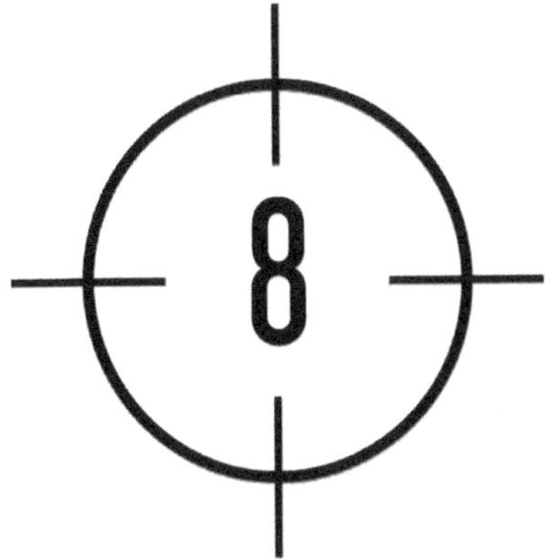

Timberview hadn't changed much in the years Maggie had been gone. They still had Mom and Pop businesses. Wal-Mart hadn't made it this far into the north. She knew it had been a long time since some of these people had seen her, but she'd been sure she could win them over. Now with this, she was beginning to wonder. How had an attack on the school suddenly become an attack on her? What was going on with Austin Howard?

Maggie was ushered into Sheriff Norton's office. He offered her some coffee as she sat down. After handing her a cup he sat behind his desk and said, "Tell me what you can about the male voices you heard in the school yesterday."

"I just heard voices. One of them was looking for me. One said he was going to take care of business and the other should find me. There was also a comment about the school being unusable," she replied thoughtfully. Then she said, "But I thought your officers didn't believe anyone was in the building."

"They believed enough to run by there about every hour. They also told the next shift to keep an eye out," he said.

"So, why was Austin Howard trying to damage the elementary school?"

"I was hoping you could tell me, Mrs. Parsons."

"Me?" she asked incredulously, "I've only been back in Timberview three weeks. I haven't seen Austin Howard since I graduated high school almost twenty years ago."

"Well, there must be something," Sheriff Norton said, "He's never done anything like this before."

"Did you know he was fired by the school district at the end of the last school year?" she asked calmly.

"No, I was not aware."

"It might be the reason he was trying to destroy a school building."

"I'll be looking into it. Now what made you come back to Timberview?"

"I didn't know I needed a reason. My mother lives here as well as my brother and his family. There was an opening for an elementary principal, I applied and was hired. What does this have to do with anything?"

"I just want to know all the players in this game."

"I don't see vandalizing a school as a game, Sheriff, nor do I see how my personal life has anything to do with it," she said indignantly.

"I'm just covering all the bases, Mrs. Parsons. Will Mr. Parsons be moving to Timberview also?"

Maggie choked on the coffee she was drinking, and then said acidly, "Not *that* it's any of your business, Mr. Parsons died three months ago." She put down the coffee cup and stood. "I think we have covered everything, Sheriff, please keep me informed about the investigation." Maggie turned and walked from the office.

Once she got to her car, Maggie just sat and fumed. What would make the Sheriff care why she came back to Timberview? How could her coming back have anything to do with the incident at the school? She called her secretary to say she would be in later in the afternoon. Then she drove home.

Maggie was surprised to find her mother was not at home. She rummaged around in the kitchen and found the makings for a salad and put on the kettle to boil water for a cup of tea. She leafed through the mail on the entry table and found one addressed to her from a realtor in Davenport. She took the envelope and walked into the kitchen as she ate she read the letter.

> Dear Mrs. Parsons,
>
> We are contacting you on behalf of a client, who is very interested in purchasing your home. I have not been able to find it listed on the market. If your home is indeed up for sale, please contact our office at your earliest convenience. Our number is 213-487-6600 please ask for me by name.
>
> Sincerely,
> Robert Baker
> Real One Real Estate
> 2400 Block Blvd, Suite 101
> Davenport, MI 49003

Sell the house!!! She hadn't even considered it. What in the world is going on? Who are these mysterious people who want to buy her home? Should she sell? What would she do with everything? Why now? Maggie suddenly felt as if her world was crashing in again. She dropped her head onto her arms and began to cry.

Which is how her mother found her. Sitting at the counter with her head in her hands and sobbing.

"Maggie, for Heaven's sake what is the problem now?" Estelle asked anxiously.

Maggie looked up through her tears and replied, "Mom, they think the vandalism last night was my fault and some real estate agent in Davenport wants to sell my house. It feels like my life is out of control. How has it come to this?"

"Let me make some more tea and see if we can sort this out," she replied. As she started to heat the water, she took out two fresh tea bags and a cup for herself. Then she turned to Maggie and said, "I just came from the Ladies Auxiliary brunch. There was much being said there about the problem at the school and Austin Howard."

"Really, Mom, gossip?" Maggie said disgustedly.

"Let me tell you what I learned," she said as she poured the water into the cups. "Austin Howard has had some problems since his wife died. He hasn't been himself. Let me think, he married the mousy little Stephens girl, what was her name? Oh, yes, Molly. She died about a year ago of cancer. He's fallen behind on his bills, has been late to work, his work has been below standard, and he's taken to drinking."

"All this means what? The the poor guy is trying to get over the loss of his wife."

"Well, they lost a couple of children at birth, so he has no family in town any more."

"Losing a wife and children sent him over the edge and made him want to destroy the elementary school?"

"Well, Maggie, from the looks of things, I'd say yes."

"Mom, it sounds like wonderful logic however; the Sheriff was asking me all kinds of personal questions, like the whole thing was my fault."

"And just what kind of questions was he asking?" Estelle said sharply.

"He wanted to know why I came back to Timberview, if I was planning to stay, and if Mr. Parsons would be joining me."

"Those questions were none of his business and he had no right asking them," she said indignantly.

"He gave the excuse, he was just being thorough."

"Well, just let me get a hold of the girls. We'll see if Sheriff Norton keeps his job doing things like that to innocent citizens."

"My concern is not with whether or not the Sheriff gets re-elected. I heard two voices in the building. Aussie did not do this alone. I wish I could talk to him."

"What nonsense. You don't need to talk to Austin Howard. He is the criminal here. He was caught red handed."

"I know. It's just very frustrating." Maggie shook her head and finished her cup of tea. Then she said, "I'm going to go freshen up. I need to go back to the school for a couple of hours. The teachers are all going to come in for a meeting."

"What about this real estate agent?" Estelle asked.

"I'm not going to deal with him right now. I will do it later. The first order of business is to get the school ready for the kids next week," Maggie marched off to the bathroom to ready herself for the meeting ahead.

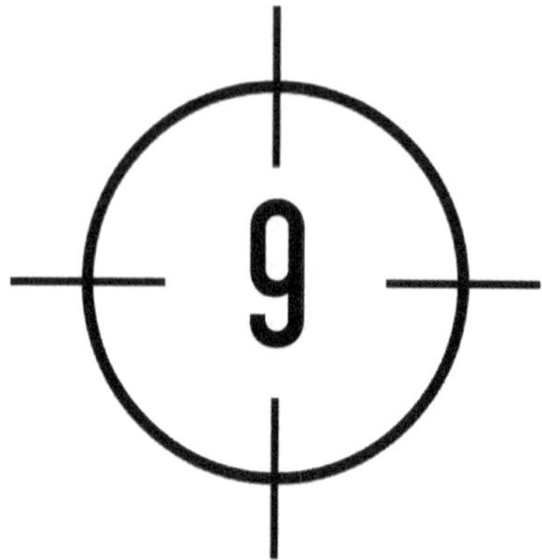

By the time she reached the school, Maggie was in control of her emotions. The teachers had gathered in the lounge. Maggie had met them all at different times when they had come in to ready their rooms. They were a good group. She explained to them everything which had transpired yesterday up to the time the police called because they had caught someone vandalizing the school.

"As you can see the vandalism was mostly in the halls and stairwells. Bob Addison assures me this will be cleaned up by tomorrow and we will be ready to open next week. I am going to ask if you plan to come into the building to work you only come during the day when the secretary and I are here. I'd also like you to come in pairs. I don't want someone working alone and trapped if something else should happen. Are there any questions?"

"Mrs. Parsons, doesn't it seem a bit extreme?" asked Ginny Barnes one of the kindergarten teachers.

"It would if I hadn't heard two voices. The police only have one man in custody."

"Are you expecting more trouble?" Ida Waters asked.

"As I said, I heard two voices. I am hoping there will be no more problems, however I am erring on the side of caution until this is all resolved."

"Will you be working alone?" Brett Anderson wanted to know.

"Not anymore. I will have the hours of a regular school day."

"I'm glad you weren't hurt," Alice Wixom volunteered.

There was a chorus of agreement.

"Thank you for your concern. If there are no more questions, you are free to leave. I want to thank you for coming in at such short notice."

Many people milled around talking and Brett Anderson made a sweep of the building after all the teachers left. He stopped in at the office on his way out. Hope Cassidy, the secretary, was at her desk. She was a full-figured five feet two inch dynamo who kept her sandy hair in a short bouncy bob.

"What can I do for you, Brett?" she asked.

"Nothing just let Mrs. Parsons know I did a sweep of the building. The two of you are the only ones left. Have a good evening." He turned and left the building.

Hope walked into Maggie's office, "Did you hear Brett Anderson?"

"I heard him out there, but I was on the phone. Did he want something?"

"He wanted you to know he has done a sweep of the building and we are the only ones left," Hope said rolling her eyes.

"Which was nice of him," Maggie replied distractedly.

"Nice! Maggie, he is trying to make points with you."

Maggie looked up from what she'd been doing, "Make points? I plan to treat all the teachers equally."

Hope giggled. "You have been out of circulation too long, Girl. He is building up to hitting on you."

Maggie blushed. "Well, it is out of the question. I won't be dating my staff. What do you say we call it a day?"

"Works for me, Boss," Hope replied as she headed toward her desk to get her purse, put the phones on auto response and shut down her computer.

By the time Hope was done, Maggie had joined her and the two locked up and walked out together.

"Hope," Maggie said as she reached her car, "thanks for getting everyone in on a Saturday."

Hope smiled and said, "All in a day's work." Then got into her car and drove off.

Maggie was not looking forward to discussing her afternoon or the real estate agent with her mother when she got home. She was very surprised to find a note on the table. The note read:

> Maggie,
>
> I have gone to visit Margie Beecham. She has been doing poorly for the past couple of weeks. I left some stew in the oven for you. Rest up as I promised your brother we would be there for dinner tomorrow after church. The kids are really looking forward to seeing you.
>
> Love,
> Mother
> xoxox

Maggie decided she would take a warm bath, have her dinner, then curl up with a good book. It sounded exactly like the evening she needed if she was going to spend tomorrow with her nieces and nephews. She smiled as she went to the bathroom to start the water running. She went to her bedroom, stripped off her clothes, put on her robe, and carried her pajamas to the bathroom. She eased herself into the warm water and closed her eyes. When the water started getting cold she soaped herself up, rinsed off and climbed out of the tub. After draining the tub, drying off, and dressing in her pajamas, she went to the kitchen for dinner. She was just finishing the dishes when her mother came in.

"*That* miserable old woman!" Estelle sputtered, "You'd think I was her maid, the way she treated me was appalling."

Maggie smiled. This was her mother's reaction every time she came back from visiting a sick friend. Maggie thought of it as her mother's defense against growing older. She dutifully responded saying, "What on earth did Mrs. Beecham do?"

"You can just stop patronizing me," her mother scolded. "I go to see Margie out of the goodness of my heart and all she can do is give me orders like I am her lackey. Estelle, make me some tea. Estelle, fluff my pillows. Estelle, can you please read to me? And on and on the whole time I was there."

"Didn't you go over to offer her comfort?" Maggie quipped.

"Of course I did, don't be pert," Estelle said tersely. "I had hoped she would ask about you, or the incident at the school. She didn't care about anything but herself."

"Oh, Mom, she's not feeling well, so she's not herself. Give her a day or two and go again."

"I guess you're right. Now, what are you planning to do for the rest of the evening?" Estelle asked hopefully.

"I've got a book I'm trying to finish before school starts. I'm going to read in bed and then go to sleep. Have a good evening, Mom."

"Hrrmph," Estelle muttered as Maggie left the room, "good evening indeed. Even my own daughter is avoiding me. Well, she won't be able to avoid me tomorrow."

Both women retired to their rooms, Estelle to brood and Maggie to read before falling asleep.

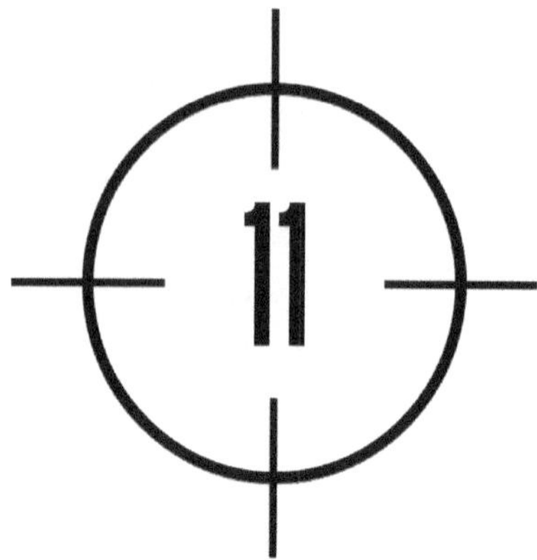

Sunday was like any other morning for Maggie. She started out with her morning run. She came back and showered before she joined her mother in the kitchen. Estelle had breakfast ready. She brought the coffee to the table and handed Maggie a cup as she sat down.

"Maggie, are you planning to wear slacks to church?" she inquired.

"Yes, I will be wearing a suit. Is it a problem?"

"In my day one always wore a dress to church," her mother sniffed.

"Mom, things have changed. I am not wearing blue jeans although I am sure there maybe someone there who does. God does not care what I am wearing, he cares what I believe."

"Well, it is true; however as the new principal in town I would think you would want to make a good impression."

"Most of the people at the church watched me grow up. Many of them will remember the kind of girl I was. I have nothing to prove about who I am."

"Are you planning to change before we go to your brother's?

"No, Mom, I thought we were going there right after the service," Maggie said in an exasperated tone.

"I had hoped we would just follow him home."

"Then it is what we will do." Finishing her breakfast, Maggie took her dishes to the sink. "I will wash the dishes, so you can finish getting ready."

"Thank you, dear," Estelle replied.

Maggie quickly did the dishes. She wondered how long she would be able to tolerate living with her mother. They had not been the best of friends when she was growing up. Dad had been the peacemaker when they were at odds. She missed him. She shook her head out of her reverie as her mother entered the kitchen. "All set?" she asked.

"Yes."

"Well, then let's be off."

The ride to the church was short. They joined her brother Martin and his family and went inside. The service was nice. Maggie liked they were now doing a children's sermon so the children would understand the Bible and its stories. Once the children left for their classes the minister began the adult sermon. Today's sermon was on forgiveness.

When the service was over they spoke to friends. Many told Maggie how sorry they were about the incident at the school. As soon as she could she left those milling about and made her way to the cemetery. She stood for a few minutes at her father's grave. She thought of all the times he'd stood by her while she was growing up. She sensed Martin coming up beside her. He said nothing and took her hand.

She lifted her eyes to his identical blue ones and said, "I miss him so much."

"I know, I do too," he said then added, "Mother wants to ride with Ellen and I, do you mind having the kids with you?"

She laughed, "Never, they are great company."

"You're sure it won't be too hard?"

"I'm sure."

"Ok, let's get everyone rounded up."

Together they went toward the front of the church to find the rest of their family. Josh, Elyssa, and Abby rode with her. Josh wanted the front seat as he was the oldest. Estelle rode with Martin and Ellen and baby Wyatt. The drive to Martin's house was uneventful. Once there the kids ran to their rooms to change clothes and Maggie went to see if she could help in the kitchen. Estelle made herself at home in the living room and Martin went to find some coffee.

Ellen fixed a nice meal of roasted chicken, mashed potatoes, gravy, salad, and mixed vegetables with apple crisp and ice cream for dessert. The meal was pleasant and the children kept the conversation lively. Maggie was able to sit back and enjoy herself. After dinner she and Ellen did the dishes. When they were done she made her way to the backyard to spend some time with her nieces and nephew.

Estelle called Ellen and Martin into the living room. "Something has to be done about Maggie," she said bluntly.

"Mother, Maggie is a grown woman," Martin said.

"Yes, but she has horrible nightmares. It just about scares me to death when she screams at the top of her lungs in the middle of the night. She won't talk about them, just has some milk and goes back to sleep, and now there is this mess at the school."

"The mess at the school is not Maggie's fault," Martin said, "and as to her nightmares, she just lost a husband and two children. It would give me nightmares. I'm not sure I would want to talk about it either."

Ellen shivered and said, "I think she is very strong."

"Well, strong or not I found her crying in the kitchen yesterday. Someone has made an offer for her house. She doesn't even know if she wants to sell it and the police seem to think she is the reason for the attack on the school."

"Why on earth would they think so?" asked a shocked Ellen.

"She dated Austin Howard in high school and everyone knows it."

"Mom, high school was almost twenty years ago. They were just kids. It has nothing to do with this."

"Well, the police questioned Maggie like it did."

"Let the police do their jobs. Maggie will be fine. Just leave her alone."

"I really think she should stop her early morning running. It just isn't seemly," Estelle said determinedly.

"For crying out loud" Martin shouted throwing his hands in the air in frustration, "this is the twenty-first century! Women run at all hours of the day. It's exercise, Mom, not adultery or some criminal activity." Exasperated Martin left the room to join his sister and children in the backyard.

"You can't think it's right, Ellen," Estelle encouraged.

"Well," Ellen hesitated not wanting to offend her mother-in-law, "I wouldn't do it."

"Of course you wouldn't, dear, you know what it is to be respectable in Timberview," Estelle said patting her hand.

Ellen was a timid woman with mousy brown hair and dull brown eyes, who loved her husband with all her heart. She was intimidated by her mother-in-law and frequently bowed to her judgment even if she disagreed. This was one of those times.

They were interrupted by twelve year old Josh exploding into the room, "Mom, you've got to come!" he shouted, "Elyssa and Aunt Maggie are having a water fight with the hose!" He turned and exited as quickly as he came in.

"Oh, honestly," said a disgusted Estelle.

The two women went to the backyard to see what was going on, by this time Josh, Martin, and Abby had joined in. Ellen smiled behind her hand wishing she had the courage to join them.

"Martin, Maggie, stop at once!" Estelle shouted.

All of the laughter ceased. Everyone looked at Estelle, who stood with her hands on her hips and a disapproving look on her face.

Maggie put the hose down and said, "Martin do you have a couple of towels you can spare? I'm going to need to dry off before I go home." She turned to the children and said, "Maybe we can do this again sometime." She winked.

The children came running toward her and threw their wet bodies against her begging, "Please don't leave, Aunt Maggie, please."

"I don't live too far away. I'll come back soon," she said extricating herself and reaching for the towels Ellen handed her.

"Maggie, I have a pair of jeans and a shirt you can change into if you'd like," Ellen offered, "they might be a bit short, but they're dry."

"Thanks, Ellen, I'd love to." She went inside with Ellen to change.

Maggie was quiet on the way home. Estelle finally broke the silence, "You should behave with more decorum. After all you are an adult."

"Mom, I'm not going to argue with you. We don't agree on many things and this is one of them."

"Well then, tell me how you can forget you are in mourning?"

"I never forget what I've lost. It's with me all of the time whether I'm awake or asleep. It doesn't keep me from moving on with my life. They would have wanted it this way."

"I don't think I've ever even seen you cry over the accident," Estelle said judgmentally.

"Oh, I've cried. I've cried until I thought there were no more tears," Maggie replied. "I just don't choose to cry in public. It's my grief and I chose to deal with it in my own way."

"They were my grandchildren," Estelle said softly, "and my son-in-law."

"Yes, they were. I not only lost my two children, I lost my husband. It's a heavy burden to bear. I should have been with them," Maggie said sadly.

"NO!" Estelle shrieked, "I could not have borne it if I'd lost you, too!"

"It's not what I mean. I just mean, if I'd been with them things might have been different," Maggie said.

"You couldn't have changed what happened," said Estelle, "no matter how much you think you could have."

"I know," Maggie replied, "but it doesn't make it any easier."

"You know, I've never heard exactly what happened."

"All I know is they were pulling out of the supermarket parking lot when a drunk plowed into them at a high speed. I don't know how Ben missed seeing him; I don't know what the kids might have been doing to distract him. I just don't know. It plays over and over in my head. It's what causes the nightmares." Tears slowly fell down Maggie cheeks.

"I'm so sorry, Maggie," her mother said softly.

"I know, Mom."

They arrived at home. Maggie put her wet clothes in the laundry room and went to her bedroom. She had a headache and just wanted to lie down.

Estelle set about doing laundry then settled into her favorite chair to read the newspaper and think about what Maggie said. Somehow finally hearing her daughter talk about the accident made her feel closer to Maggie.

Maggie was up early and out running when Sheriff Norton caught up with her. She slowed to a jog as he pulled up beside her.

"Are you sure you should be out running alone?" he asked as he drove along beside her.

"Why wouldn't I be?"

"I just thought after the school incident you'd be very careful."

"Sheriff, whatever you think, the 'school incident' as you call it had nothing to do with me. I grew up in Timberview, almost everyone here knows me. Running in the morning is something I have done for years and I see no reason to stop now."

"Well, you just be careful," he said, then drove off.

Maggie wondered just what he was trying to prove. How could her running put her in danger? Austin Howard was still locked up as far as she knew; besides he had been vandalizing the school not trying to hurt her. She shook her head and started running again. She was stretching in the yard when another police cruiser drove by. What in the world is going on?

Her mother was making coffee when she entered. "I see the police are cruising by the house. Are they trying to get a good look at the new principal while she prances around in her shorts?"

"Honestly, Mother!" Maggie said exasperatedly. She headed toward the bathroom for a shower.

"What am I supposed to think?" her mother called after her.

After her shower Maggie dressed and headed to the school. She had some things to take care of and she wanted people to know the vandalism had not scared her away. When she arrived, Hope was registering a new student. She introduced the mother to Maggie.

"Not Maggie Mills?" the mother questioned.

"I was Maggie Mills, yes," she responded, "Have we met?"

"Maggie, it's me Ashton, Ashton Blake," the woman replied, "or at least I was when we were kids." She walked to Maggie with her arms held out.

Maggie quickly hugged the young woman she had spent much of her childhood chumming around with.

"It's good to see you, Ash," Maggie said. "We will have to have lunch one day and catch up. How many children do you have?"

"Two, Samantha will be in first grade and Tyler is not yet ready for school."

"So, what made you move back?"

"A divorce," Ashton replied, "things don't always work out the way you plan."

"No," Maggie agreed, "they certainly don't."

"I heard about the tragedy, Maggie, I'm really sorry," Ashton offered her condolences.

"I'm trying to put it behind me," Maggie replied, "but thank you."

"Well, I'm sure you have things to do. I won't keep you," said Ashton. "It sure was nice seeing you again."

"You, too," Maggie replied then asked, "Where are you living?"

Ashton let out a throaty laugh, "With my parents until I get a settlement. I'm hoping it won't be too long."

Maggie nodded knowing the feeling. "I'm at Mom's if you want to talk."

"Thanks, Maggie," Ashton said and turned back to the papers she was filling out.

Maggie went into her office and closed the door. Fate it seemed was bringing everyone back to Timberview. She wondered what was coming next.

Maggie, seeing Hope had made her tea, poured herself a cup, added cream and sugar; them leaned back in her chair and thought about Ashton Blake. She'd been the blonde bombshell of the cheerleading squad. She'd been homecoming queen and had gone off to college with the captain of the football team. Evidently they hadn't married and lived happily ever after. She wondered about the husband Ashton was leaving. How long had they been married? What business was he in? What had caused the breakup? They had been best friends since childhood. Ashton had dragged Maggie along in her wake. Which was how Maggie had ended up on the cheerleading squad and the homecoming court, not because Maggie wasn't attractive or popular on her own; she just followed in Ashton's wake. It had always been that way. Maggie was the serious one and Ashton was the one looking for fun and adventure. With Laura Gilbert they had made the three musketeers willing to take on all challenges.

Maggie was about five feet seven inches tall. She had wavy, chestnut colored hair she wore at shoulder length. Her eyes were a deep blue holding a sadness which made her look vulnerable. She was still slender even at thirty-seven.

She came out of her reverie with a start as the phone rang. "Hello, this is Mrs. Parsons."

"Maggie, it's Hope. There is a bit of a problem can you come out here?"

"Sure thing, I'm on my way." Maggie put down the phone and her cup of tea and walked into the outer office.

"May I help you?" she asked the back of the man in front of her.

He turned to her and said, "I'm real sorry, Mrs. Parsons, but my wife has decided to home school our kids. I really don't want to take them out of school, but she thinks they'll be safer at home."

"Would you like to come into my office and talk about this?" Maggie offered.

"If it's no trouble," he said hopefully.

"Not at all," Maggie said as she led the way into her office. "Would you like a cup of coffee?"

"It'd be real nice, Ma'm."

She handed him a cup of coffee then sat at her desk. The man seated across from her looked familiar and she found herself saying, "I'm sorry I don't know your name."

He grinned sheepishly and said, "Yes, Maggie, you do. I'm Glen Swift."

It was Maggie's turn to blush, "I remember you, Glen. Now what is the problem with your wife?"

"After the commotion here on Friday night, she thinks the kids would be safer at home."

"I can understand her fears. We are having a meeting for parents on Thursday. I had letters sent out this morning. Do you think you can put her off until after the meeting?"

"I'll do my best to try," he said, "She can be a might determined when she sets her mind to something."

"If you can get her to wait until after the meeting I think we can convince her to let the kids stay in school."

"Great! The boys have been real mad since she told them they couldn't come."

"I think we can work something out which will make everyone happy."

"Okay, I'll go home and tell her. Thank you for taking the time to talk to me."

Maggie rose, "You are welcome, Glen. I'm looking forward to seeing you and your wife on Thursday." She shook hands with him and led him to the door.

After he left, Maggie turned to Hope, "Have there been many people pulling their kids out?"

"No, he was the first and I got the impression he didn't want to."

"He's not going to until after the meeting on Thursday."

"Thank goodness."

"You are right," Maggie said. She went back into her office to finish the report she had to send to Mr. Whitehead by this afternoon. The superintendent would want to know about the parent meeting she was planning as well as what had been done in the way of security.

After a quick lunch, Hope had planned, she was back at her desk. Which was where Mrs. Feldstein found her. Mrs. Feldstein was a matronly woman with white hair. She looked grandmotherly. Her brown eyes seemed all knowing.

"I hope I'm not interrupting," she said after a timid knock on the door.

"Of course not," Maggie said as she rose from her desk, "Please come in and have a seat."

"I remember you as a teen," Mrs. Feldstein said.

"I think there are many in this town who knew me at some point in my life. Did I do something to offend you when I was a teen?"

"Heavens no!" cried Mrs. Feldstein, "You were one of the nicest young ladies, why I remember you taking groceries to Mrs. Beecham when she fell and broke her leg. I just wanted you to know, I have faith in you and I feel you will be good for our students."

"Why thank you. Please sit down and I'll get us some coffee."

Mrs. Feldstein eased herself into a chair and waited for Maggie to bring the coffee. It had been a long time ago when she watched a younger Maggie care for then recently widowed Margie Beecham. The other girls had made fun of her, yet she didn't seem to mind. It's the kind of person who should be setting an example for kids today.

Maggie handed Mrs. Feldstein a cup of coffee then took the chair next to her. "What can I do for you, Mrs. Feldstein?"

"I just thought I should stop in and show my support. Please if there is anything I can help you with which will make this job easier for you, let me know," she said.

"Right now, it's enough to know you are in my corner," Maggie responded. "I feel as though the police are somehow blaming me for the vandalism."

"Why would they want to blame you?" asked a surprised Mrs. Feldstein.

"Somehow they know I dated Austin Howard a couple of times in high school. I don't have a clue what it has to do with things now. I haven't seen Austin since we were kids."

"Well, how silly," sighed Mrs. Feldstein, "to think something which happened twenty years ago could be affecting things today. Who on earth would try to make a connection?"

"At the moment, Sheriff Norton seems to have some suspicions. I'm sure it will work out. Will you be at the parent meeting Thursday night?"

"Yes, dear, I will be there. I think the parents will find you have everything under control."

"Thank you for the vote of confidence. I have stopped Glen Swift from pulling his kids from the school until after the meeting. His wife wants to home school them."

Mrs. Feldstein choked on her coffee. When she regained her composure she said, "Ellie Swift couldn't teach a kitten how to drink milk. She's just worried because you went to school with Glen."

"Oh for goodness sakes, why does my having been a student with some of the town residents make any difference at all in the job I do?" Maggie asked exasperatedly. "This has gone too far. I am not a threat to any woman where her husband is concerned. I just lost my own."

Mrs. Feldstein patted Maggie on the hand. "It was a tragedy, I know. The town paper ran the news articles for a week. I don't know how your family could stand it. They sensationalized everything. I guess they thought you'd never come back here to live."

"Which makes sense. It also explains why everyone is interested in me. I will have to see if there are any copies of the articles so I know what I am up against. Thank you so much, Mrs. Feldstein, you've been a bigger help than you know."

Mrs. Feldstein set her cup on Maggie's desk and stood up. "I'm glad I could help." She held out her hand and shook Maggie's. Then she left the room.

Maggie sat down and just stared into space. It was starting to make sense now. She wondered what had been written. Martin might help her to find out. As she did a final sweep of the building, she thought about her brother. They were eighteen months apart in age. Although Marty was older, they were often mistaken for twins. He was six feet tall but their coloring was identical. He had been her first soul mate.

Once all the teachers left the building, Maggie and Hope collected their things and headed to their cars. Hope tried to convince Maggie to stop on the way home for a quick drink. Maggie declined and left heading toward home. She just wanted to relax and not think. It seemed all she could do was think. She took her cell phone from her purse and called Martin.

"Hi, Marty, it's Maggie," she said when he answered. "I have a favor to ask."

"Sure go ahead."

"Can you help me get back copies of the articles which ran here in Timberview when the accident happened?"

She could hear Martin's breath hiss, then he responded, "I have them all at home. I knew some day you would ask this question."

"Great! Can I come by and get them?"

"Maggie, does Mom know you are asking for these?"

"No, and she doesn't have to know. I'll just tell her I'm doing some research."

"She's gonna kill me if she finds out."

"She won't find out. I need to know what was written. I never read anything about the accident I was too busy living it. Besides, I think the key to the school thing is in there."

"Okay, I'll meet you at the house in about ten minutes."

"I'll be there, and, Marty, thanks." Maggie hung up the phone and headed for Marty and Ellen's house. She needed to return the towel, jeans and shirt she had with her anyway.

Marty hung up the phone thinking he was going to wish he hadn't told her he had the articles. Their mother was going to start raging as soon as she found out. She'd been angry he'd kept them in the first place.

Maggie and Marty arrived at about the same time. He led her into the garage and opened a brief case. Inside were several newspaper clippings. Maggie thanked him and headed toward her car. There she transferred the clippings into her own briefcase and returned Marty's to the garage. She handed him his empty briefcase and the clothes Ellen had loaned her on Sunday. Then she drove home.

"Hi, Mom," she said cheerfully as she came through the back door. "Just give me a couple of minutes to change and I'll help with dinner. I have a lot to tell you."

"I'm sure you do," Estelle said sternly.

Maggie looked at her mother, "What's wrong?"

"Go change, then we will talk about what's wrong."

"Okay," Maggie said and headed for her room. She was sure she'd hear all about it in a few minutes. When she returned to the kitchen her mother was holding a gin and tonic and had mixed Maggie a margarita. "Wow, are we having a party?"

"No, Maggie, we are not," her mother answered crossly.

"Mom, has made you so angry now?" Maggie sat on a stool and picked up her drink.

Estelle looked at her daughter and knew she was looking at a stranger. "It has come to my attention you returned to Timberview to take up with someone you knew as a child."

Maggie's jaw dropped open. "What are you talking about?"

"Mae Belle Richards at the beauty shop has heard it and made sure to tell me when I was in for my weekly manicure. The rumor has it you've been carrying a torch for someone in town and it's what brought you back. When were you going to tell me?"

"I'm not sure where Mae Belle got her information, but it's not even close to correct. Mom, I loved Ben and only Ben. Part of me died in the accident with him. I came back here because I felt safe here. I could not face living in our house without him or the children. The house felt empty and I kept seeing them everywhere. If you are going to continue to listen to town gossip, I am going to find a place of my own to live."

"It might be a good idea. Do you want to tell me why Glen Swift was in your office today?"

"Which was part of what I was going to tell you. Do you want It first or my other news?"

"I asked about Glen."

"Glen has two children who attend school at the elementary. His wife was worried about their safety and wanted Glen to withdraw them from the school, so she could homeschool them. I told him to bring his wife to the meeting on Thursday night and then make a decision. He agreed. Are you satisfied?"

Estelle took a sip of her drink. "If you're sure there was nothing more."

"I'm sure. Why would there be anything more?"

"But you were late coming home tonight."

"I stopped by to see Marty. I wanted his thoughts on this whole thing."

"You could have called," Estelle whined.

"I'm sorry, I should have," Maggie said apologetically. "I have some other news. Ashton Blake has moved in with her parents. She and her two kids are living there. She was enrolling her daughter in school today."

"Ashton is back? What happened to her husband?"

"I believe she said they were getting a divorce."

"Oh, my, Helene will be devastated. At least you're a widow and not a divorcee."

"Really, Mother, some marriages just don't work out. It seems like Ashton's was one of them."

"Did she give you any details?"

"She only said she is expecting a large settlement."

"Hmmm, it will give me something to look into."

"You enjoy yourself. Now what is for dinner, I'm starved?"

Estelle quickly got a tuna noodle salad out of the refrigerator and set it on the counter. Then she pulled some rolls from the oven where they had been warming.

"This looks great! Are we eating at the counter tonight?"

"I think it would be nice," Estelle agreed.

Maggie quickly set the counter for two and they sat down to a pleasant meal. After washing the dishes, Maggie told her mother, she had some work to do so she was going to her room.

"It will be fine, dear," Estelle replied. She was busy with her address book thinking of ladies she could call and invite for luncheon tomorrow. Ashton Blake and her mother would be among the guests.

Maggie settled into her bed and took out the clippings Marty had given her. The first one wasn't too bad. The headline read: LOCAL FAMILY STRUCK BY TRAGEDY. It went on to tell how the family of Estelle Mills had been wiped out in an auto accident. Some of the others were a bit more sensational. One had even caught a photo of Maggie showing her with a blank look in her eyes. The headline read FORMER RESIDENT DRUGGED IN ORDER TO FACE ORDEAL. The thing which got her the most was the drunk driver and his car had disappeared. It's like they were never there. Yet she had seen the wreckage of the car her family had been in. Police had no leads. After reading all of the articles she turned out the lights and went to sleep.

Estelle heard the first of the screams at around 2 a.m. She knew Maggie was having another of her nightmares. Quickly she got up, put on her robe, and went to Maggie's room. She flipped on the light and saw all of the clippings on the floor. Maggie was screaming and thrashing in the bed. Estelle went to her and held her all the while talking softly as if to a small child. When the terror subsided and Maggie was more lucid, Estelle said, "I'll make some tea."

She went to the kitchen and put the kettle on. Maggie wandered out a few minutes later. When Estelle set the tea in front of Maggie, she said, "Didn't you think about what those articles would do? Why would you even want to read them?"

"I didn't read them when it happened. I didn't know the driver had just driven away. How can it be? I saw our car. I thought he or she had died, too. Oh, Mom, this is awful!" Maggie hung her head and cried.

"I'm sorry, Maggie, I really thought you knew. Do you think we should hire someone to look into it?"

"I wouldn't know who to hire," Maggie said regretfully.

"I think I might. You father knew a man in Slate Rock, once who did the kind of work. I'll call him in the morning. If he is retired, he might be able to recommend someone else."

"Thanks, Mom. I'm so sorry I woke you again."

"It's okay. Now let's see if we can get some sleep."

The two women went back to their bedrooms. Maggie bent down and picked up all the clippings. She put them on the dresser. Then she turned off the light and slept the sleep of the dreamless.

Estelle crawled into bed and picked up her address book from the night stand. She fingered through it until she found the name she was looking for. It would be the first thing she did after breakfast in the morning. Maggie needed closure to move forward. Then she turned out the light and tried to go back to sleep.

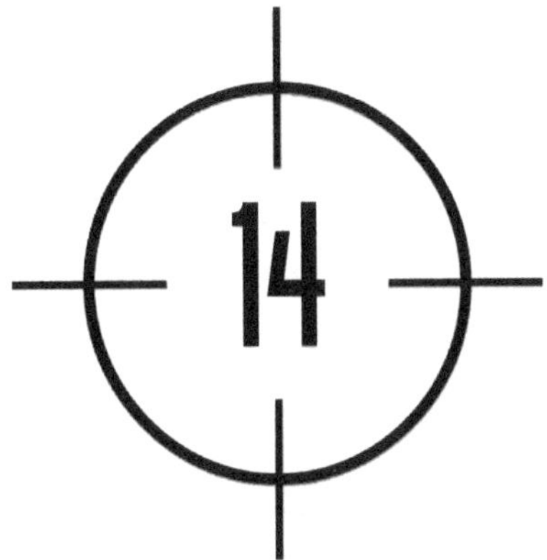


Estelle had seen Maggie off and was now ready to begin her phone calls. She started with Robert's old friend, Don Adler. He could point her in the direction of an investigator.

"Hello," said a raspy voice.

"Hello, Don, this is Estelle Mills. How are you?"

"Estelle, I'm doing okay, been retired for a couple of years."

"I was wondering if you knew anyone doing investigating these days?"

"Sure, I know a couple of people. What do you need investigated?"

"My daughter's husband and children were killed by a drunk driver about three months ago. The police have no leads."

"I'm sorry Estelle. Did the driver walk away?"

"No, apparently the person drove away. No one saw it happen and no car was at the scene other than my son-in-laws."

"Hmmm, I'll check to see who the best person is for accident investigation. How soon do you want to start?"

"As soon as possible, do you think you could have someone by dinner time?"

"For you, Estelle, I can have someone by lunch."

"You find this person and bring him to dinner at six."

"Would there be a problem if the person is a woman?"

"Not if she is the best."

"I only work with the best. I'll find someone and we'll be there at six. I'm looking forward to seeing you again."

"Thanks, Don, see you soon."

Having finished one item on her list, Estelle made a second cup of coffee and started calling ladies for her impromptu luncheon. She also called Rosa at the deli and ordered a summer luncheon tray. Then she took a leisurely bath and set the table. The delivery boy from the deli arrived promptly at eleven thirty. Estelle took the food and put it out on her fine luncheon china. She made some lemonade and everything was ready. Her guests would be arriving soon.

stelle greeted everyone and ushered them into the dining room. The table was set and the ladies could serve themselves at the counter. When everyone was seated Estelle asked Elizabeth Winters if she would give the blessing. Being the minister's wife she was asked to do this a lot. Once it was done the chatter began.

Estelle started off by introducing Ashton, "Ladies, I'd like you to meet one of Maggie's dearest friends, Ashton Blake. Oh, Aston, I'm so sorry I don't remember your married name."

"It's ok Mrs. Mills," she said as she looked at the group, "my married name is Blythe."

"Of the Madison Blythes?" asked one woman.

"Yes, my husband is from Madison."

"Oh, it must be nice to live in such splendor. How long will you be visiting Timberview?" another asked.

"I have moved back here permanently," Ashton answered with a blush.

Amanda Blake wishing to turn the focus off her errant daughter asked, "Estelle, have they learned any more about the break in at the school?"

Estelle floundered for only a moment before she answered, "It seems Austin Howard was dismissed from the school last spring. I think the answer probably lies there."

"Oh, I thought Maggie might have had some updated information," Amanda said disappointedly.

"She has been in touch with Sheriff Norton and he will keep her informed of all the necessary information," Estelle said with authority. Then she turned back to Ashton, "Maggie tells me you were enrolling a child in her building."

"Yes, my daughter, Samantha will be in the first grade."

"Oh, do you have pictures?" someone asked.

Ashton reached for her purse, "I'd love to show them to you. Tyler is just turning three." She pulled out a small photo album and passed it down the table.

Everyone made complimentary comments about the two children. Then someone said, "It must be so nice for you, Amanda, to have your grandchildren with you." There was a slight rustling of table cloth then the speaker said, "Ouch!"

"Is everything all right, dear," Estelle asked.

"Yes, I must have bumped someone's leg. I'm terribly sorry," she said to the unknown person who had kicked her under the table.

"Well, Ashton, if you have any time on your hands we have a literary club which meets once a week. We'd love to have you join," invited Estelle.

There was a chorus of agreement and the meal continued. Mostly there was gossip and speculation about the school break in. There was much speculation about Austin Howard and what had gotten into him. Ashton was almost in the clear when Elizabeth Winters asked innocently, "Will we be seeing your husband in church with the rest of you on Sunday?"

Ashton choked then said, "No, Steven will not be joining us. He and I are getting a divorce." She held her breath waiting for someone to say something.

The silence was alive with expectation when Elizabeth finally said, "I'm so sorry, Dear. I wasn't meaning to pry."

"No harm done, Mrs. Winters. Now if you will all excuse me, I need to get home to my children." So saying, Ashton and her mother rose and left.

Everyone else took it as their cue to end the luncheon. They thanked Estelle on their way out. Estelle wasted no time on reflection and set about clearing up the lunch dishes and getting ready for dinner.

She had thought of everything, a nice crisp salad, steaks on the grill, some fresh corn on the cob, and a fruit parfait for dessert. She had beer for Donald, wine and mixes for everyone else. She wondered who Donald might have been able to find to investigate the accident. She also wondered how Maggie was going to react.

Once everything was ready Estelle went to her room to change clothes. She wanted to look fresh for her dinner guests. Besides, Maggie would be home soon and she would want to use the shower.

It had been a routine day for Maggie. She was looking forward to a quiet evening. Maybe she would suggest taking her mother to the concert in the park. It was all Hope could talk about this afternoon. How everyone takes blankets and lawn chairs and goes to the park to listen to an evening of music for free. It would be a nice change and give her a chance to mingle with people in town.

She was surprised to see her mother had the grill heating. It was something she usually left for Maggie to do. She hadn't mentioned a cookout. Oh well, it would be nice before going to the park.

"Hello, Maggie," her mother greeted her as she came through the door.

"Hi, Mom," Maggie said, "my, aren't you dressed up. Have you got a friend coming over for dinner?"

"We have guests coming, yes. Why don't you run along and take a shower. Please dress for dinner."

"What's going on?" Maggie asked suspiciously.

"Nothing, Don Adler and a friend are coming by for dinner. Now please go get ready."

Maggie went to her room, stripped, put on her robe, and headed for the shower. She did not like this at all. It was not the way she wanted to spend her evening. She showered quickly and returned to her room to find something suitable for dinner. She spent a good thirty minutes finding a pale blue cotton skirt with a matching peasant styled blouse. She chose to leave her hair down. In the closet she found a pair of sandals she'd purchased on the spur of the moment when she and Ben had spent a week-end in Mexico. She closed her eyes and willed the memory to fade. She did not need this tonight. What she needed was a concert in the park and no worries. Somehow she thought this surprise evening could bring some worries.

Estelle looked up from the salad she was making when Maggie entered the kitchen. "You're rather casual aren't you?" she asked upon seeing Maggie's attire.

"You didn't say it was a formal dinner. I just want to be comfortable," Maggie replied as she reached for the dinner plates.

"Please use the china," Estelle said.

"Okay, Mom, are you going to tell me why our mystery guests are coming before they arrive?" Maggie asked suspiciously.

"I have invited Don Adler to join us and he is bringing one of his associates."

"Oh, I didn't know you had a business dinner in mind. Should I change?"

"No, it's too late now. Besides, Don is an old friend."

Maggie nodded and set about putting the fine china and silverware on the table. Then she asked, "Is there anything else I can do?"

"No, I will put the corn on when we start grilling the steaks."

Maggie nodded and walked into the living room. She smiled as she looked at the familiar furniture. She could picture her father in his favorite chair reading the evening news, with a cocktail on the stand beside the chair. Her mother preferred a straight back chair with a pillow behind her. Maggie had loved sitting on the old woven rug her grandmother had made, while Marty lounged on the couch which had grown too short for him. The room had a comfortable lived in feel. She picked up the evening paper and sat on the floor. It's where Estelle found her when their guests arrived.

"For goodness sake, Margaret, you are not a child anymore get up from the floor," Estelle said with a touch of annoyance.

Maggie stood and reached for Don Adler's hand in greeting. "Hello, Don, it's been a long time."

"Hello, Maggie, I'd like you to meet, Erika Estwick, one of my colleagues."

Maggie turned to Erika with her hand outstretched. "I'm pleased to meet you."

Erika shook hands with Maggie and replied, "Likewise, I'm sure.

Erika had striking good looks, with jet black hair pulled up into a bun on the top of her head and dark brown eyes giving the impression she could look right through you. She was dressed in a pale yellow pant suit which made her dark looks even more stunning. Maggie was conscious of having under dressed for the evening.

Estelle broke the silence saying, "What can I get people to drink?"

"You know me, Estelle, I'm a beer man," Don said chuckling.

"I'll take a glass of wine if you have it," replied Erika hesitantly.

"I have a wonderful merlot," Estelle said.

"It will be fine."

"Good, and you Maggie, dear," Estelle asked.

"I'd like a Manhattan, but I'll fix mine."

Maggie and Estelle departed for the kitchen. Don and Erika made themselves at home.

"Mother, why do you need an investigator?"

"I don't, dear, you do."

"What are you talking about? The police are handling the school vandalism," Maggie whispered angrily. "You need to stay out of it."

"I'm not worried about the school vandalism. I am worried about who killed my family. No one has ever been caught. No one has ever been questioned. Doesn't it bother you?"

"I try not to think about it. I keep hoping the police will turn up some new evidence."

"Well, I think it's time we lit a fire. Besides we talked about hiring someone this morning?

"I thought it was something we were going to consider."

"We are," Estelle said, "now come along let's not ignore our guests."

Maggie took a sip of her drink and rolled her eyes. The two women walked back into the living room. Estelle handed Erika a glass of wine and Don a bottle of beer. She took her own gin and tonic and went to her chair. Maggie took another sip of her Manhattan and promptly sat on the floor. The woven rug seemed to give her a grounded feeling. She ignored her mother's frown.

Don took a swig of his beer and began, "I understand, Maggie, there have been no leads into who ran into your family."

Maggie just nodded. She had this numb feeling, like things around her were spinning out of control and she didn't know why. It had been this way when they told her, her family was all dead.

"I've talked to Erika and she has been able to get a hold of everything she could on the case. I'd like her to present it to you and then we'll decide where to go from there. Does this sound okay to you?"

"Sure, I guess," Maggie said hesitantly as she looked from Don to Erika and back to Erika again.

Erika began, "Maggie, may I call you Maggie?" When Maggie just nodded she continued, "There are several ways we can look at the evidence. The thing which bothers me most is there are no skid marks. The person who hit your husband's car did not try to slow down."

Maggie gasped. The room seemed to be spinning. It had never occurred to her someone did this on purpose. Maggie tried to refocus, she was aware Erika was still speaking.

"I'd like to look into your husband's background and business acquaintances, and then I will need to do the same with yours. Will it present a problem?" she asked.

"I can't see where it would. Ben worked in an investment firm with two other men, Jack Westin and Bill Scott," Maggie could not believe she was answering so calmly. "I will tell you anything I can about my background and the people I know."

"I just need your permission. I don't need to ask you any questions at this point. I want to look at things the police didn't."

"What things?" Estelle asked.

"I want to start with who would want to harm Ben or Maggie and why. I don't believe this had anything to do with the kids, I think they were innocent bystanders."

"Which makes sense, don't you think, Maggie?"

"I cannot imagine someone we knew would want to harm us."

"I'm sure no one you knew did this, but someone who was a passing acquaintance might have. Besides stranger things have happened, maybe you had a stalker and didn't know it."

"Since we have a plan," Don interjected, "I say we get down to the business of dinner."

He and Estelle went to grill the steaks, and she put the corn on. Maggie and Erika stayed in the living room.

"I know this has been devastating for you, Maggie. I feel there is something not right with all of this," Erika said.

"I'm sure you are right," Maggie replied, "I just haven't wanted to deal with it. So, how much is all this work going to cost me?" She looked into Erika's dark eyes.

"Let's start with tonight's dinner. I need to see if there is anything here. Once I've established there is something to investigate, then I have an hourly fee and will send you a contract."

"It sounds reasonable," Maggie said, "how about another drink?"

"I'll wait, but you feel free to have one."

Maggie grinned, "Thanks I will."

Dinner was pleasant. Don and Erika left as soon as it was done. As they were washing the dishes Maggie asked, "Mom, how would you like to go to the concert in the park tonight?"

"It would be lovely, Maggie!" Estelle exclaimed.

"I'll finish washing the dishes, why don't you go change," Maggie said.

"Thank you," Estelle said as she left the room.

When Estelle returned dressed in slacks and a blouse with a sweater thrown over her shoulders, Maggie had a blanket and a lawn chair already in the car. "Do you want to take a bottle of wine and some glasses?" she asked.

"Do you think it's a good idea since you are the school principal and you're the one driving?"

"Good point; do we have any soft drinks?"

"I'll grab a couple."

The two of them headed off toward the park for an evening of music. It was the most relaxed evening they had shared since Maggie arrived. Many of the town people stopped to chat with either Estelle or Maggie. Maggie saw Ashton with her children and waved. Ashton waved back. As Maggie listened to the music, she let thoughts about break-ins, accidents, and investigators slip from her mind. She let the music and sounds around her soothe her soul.

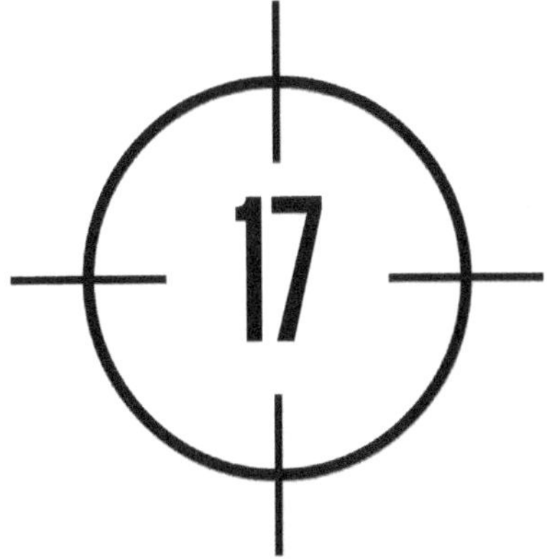

Maggie woke refreshed the next morning and set out on her run. Estelle had breakfast cooking when she returned. For once she did not scold Maggie for her morning run.

"I'll be there as soon as I shower and change, Mom," Maggie said as she went through the kitchen.

"No rush.

Maggie quickly showered and dressed for work. Then she returned to the kitchen. She sat at the counter and her mother poured her a cup of tea and a glass of orange juice.

"Thanks, Mom," Maggie said, "You are awfully quiet."

Estelle put the plate of eggs in front of Maggie and said absently, "I'm sorry, dear; I didn't mean to ignore you."

"Is something bothering you?"

"Not really, I was just thinking last night was the nicest time you and I have had since the birth of the twins. I was wishing we could do it more often."

Maggie smiled. "I'd like it, too."

"Well, we'll just have to work on it. Did I tell you about the luncheon yesterday?"

"No, I don't believe you did."

"It was all very nice, until Elizabeth asked Ashton if her husband was going to attend church with her."

"Oh, no she didn't!"

"Ashton handled it very well; unfortunately she left shortly after."

"Do you really blame her?"

"No, and it worked out nicely. I had plenty of time to prepare for dinner."

Maggie grinned such little things amused her mother. Then she said, "I need to get to work." She left the kitchen headed for her car.

Once at school, Maggie took a walk through the building. She had taken to doing it every morning so she knew who was in the building and it let her know things were still okay. Then she proceeded to her office where Hope brought her up to speed on the day ahead.

Hope was registering another child when Maggie walked into the office. "Here is our principal now. Mrs. Parsons, I'd like you to meet Mrs. Mitchell. Her son, Brandon, is in the fourth grade, Jacob is in first and her daughter, Melanie will be attending school here this year."

"I'm very pleased to meet you. Did Hope tell you about our parent meeting on Thursday night?" Maggie said with a smile.

"She did and my husband and I will be here. It's very nice to meet you too, Mrs. Parsons. My husband cannot stop talking about you."

Maggie raised her eyebrows, "I hope *that* is a good thing."

"You probably don't remember him, he's Matt Mitchell. He said he went to school with you."

"Yes, he did," Maggie replied. "I remember him. It seems to me he was on the track team."

"Why yes, he was," Mrs. Mitchell said surprised, "He'll be thrilled to know you remembered."

"I look forward to seeing you both on Thursday."

Hope chimed in and said, "These are the last of the papers you'll need, Mrs. Mitchell." Mrs. Mitchell turned to Hope, signed the papers indicated and left with the papers she had in her hands.

"Gee, everyone seems to have gone to school with you," Hope commented.

"Yes, and I have to wonder what is bringing them all back to Timberview now." Maggie walked into her office to check her in basket and begin the day's work.

She was very puzzled by all of her classmates returning to Timberview. She wondered if this was something Erika should know. She reached for her purse and Erika's business card. Then she put through the call.

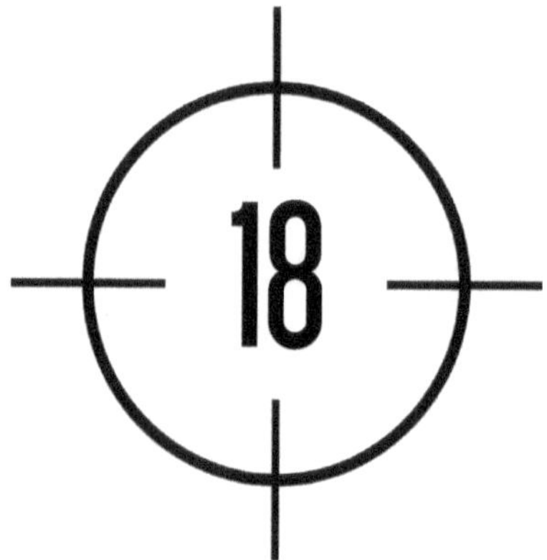



This is E and E Investigations, how may I help you?" the receptionist said into the phone.

"This is Maggie Parsons. I was wondering if I could speak to Erika Estwick."

"One moment please, while I see if she is in yet."

Maggie found herself listening to elevator music while she waited. She shuffled through the calls which had come in this morning to see who needed to be called first.

"Maggie, I'm sorry to keep you waiting," Erika said briskly. "What can I do for you this morning?"

"It may be nothing, but it seems strange to me, after twenty years away several of my classmates are returning to Timberview."

"By several how many do you mean?"

"Well, Austin Howard never left. He broke into the school a couple of nights ago. Glen Swift has children in the school. Ashton Blythe, who was my best friend, is now back after a divorce and this morning Matt Mitchell's wife enrolled their two children. It just seems strange everyone is back here at this time," Maggie said quickly. "Maybe I've just become paranoid."

"I'm sure you're not paranoid. I will look into this when I get to your background. For the moment, just go with the flow and enjoy your old friends."

"Thanks, Erika, I'll try," Maggie said. Then she hung up the phone. She shook her head. Maybe she was having fantasies; now it was time to get back to the work at hand.

At about noon, Hope came in to see if Maggie was taking a break for lunch. "I hadn't thought about it," Maggie said, "Do you know of a good restaurant?"

"I can think of several. My favorite is the Diner."

"Oh, I haven't been there since I was a teen. Would you like to go? I'm buying."

"Sure, let me put the message on the phone."

"Take your time, I need to walk through the building and let anyone here know the office is closed."

"Awesome, this will be great!"

Having made the decision, Maggie started her midday walk through the building. She found Ida Waters and Ginny Barnes in their rooms. She told them both she and Hope were going to lunch and asked if they'd like to come along. Neither took her up on her offer. Hope was waiting when she got back to the office.

"I asked both Ida Waters and Ginny Barnes to join us," Maggie said.

"Are they coming?"

"Nope, neither of them wanted to take a lunch break. It's just the two of us."

"I'll drive," Hope offered.

"Okay by me."

The two headed to the Diner for lunch. It was pretty packed when they arrived. Hope spotted a booth toward the back. They made their way to the back and the waitress followed them with menus. "What will you have to drink?" she asked.

"I'll have iced tea with lemon," Maggie replied.

"I'll have a Coke with light ice."

"Will you be wanting separate checks?" the waitress asked.

"No, put them all on one," Maggie replied.

"I'll be right back with your drinks and take your orders." She walked away.

Hope and Maggie studied the menu. "I see it hasn't changed much," Maggie commented. The décor hadn't changed much either, the red and white vinyl table cloths and red booths were still there, but a bit more worn. Maggie was sure if she put her hand under the table she'd find twenty years worth of gum stuck there.

"Nope, just your usual greasy spoon stuff; what sounds good to you?"

"I was hoping for a cob salad, but I love grilled chicken sandwiches."

"It sounds great! Shall we split an order of onion rings?"

"Mmm, I haven't had those in years. Are they as good as they used to be?"

"They sure are."

The waitress returned with their drinks, took their order and walked away. Hope found two quarters and put them in the table top juke box. "What do you want to hear?"

"Surprise me," Maggie replied.

Hope picked a couple of tunes. The first to play was Dolly Parton's "Nine to Five." Which made Maggie chuckle.

"Hey, let me in on the joke," Hope said brightly.

Maggie related how she, Ashton, and Laura Gilbert had pretended to sing along whenever the song played. They had all been confident they would have nine to five careers which would pay big money.

They laughed and they chatted until their food arrived. It was just as good as Maggie remembered. Hope's second choice of songs came on as they were finishing up. It was The

Captain and Tennille singing "Muskrat Love." Maggie stiffened at the first notes.

Hope sensed something was wrong and suggested they finish their meal and head back to the school. Maggie agreed and they finished in silence and paid the bill and left.

In the car Hope said, "I'm sorry, Maggie. I didn't mean for the song to upset you."

"It's not your fault. I am going to have to learn not to be so sensitive. Ben used to sing it too me all the time. He had a beautiful voice," Maggie said quietly.

"I never hear you talk about your family and I don't want to pry, but if you ever feel like you need to unload, I'll listen," Hope said sympathetically.

Maggie sniffed and replied, "I appreciate it, Hope, I really do, and I just am not able to talk about it at this point in my life."

"I'd like to say I understand, but I've never been in your situation. I am a good listener though."

"I know and I do appreciate it. Maybe when all this vandalism stuff is behind us and we are settled into a routine, we'll go out and get good and drunk and I'll tell you all about it."

"You've got a date."

They pulled into the parking lot to find it filled with cars.

"What now?" Maggie asked.

"Beats me," Hope replied with a grin on her face.

The two of them entered the building to see what was going on. They found the entire staff busy in the multipurpose room. The teachers were setting up chairs, hanging signs and getting ready for the meeting later this week. Hope slipped off to the office grinning. Maggie was completely overwhelmed and could not stop the tears from rolling down her cheeks.

"It was Mrs. Feldstein's idea," Ginny said as she walked toward Maggie. "I hope it's okay."

Maggie laughed, "Okay. It's terrific!" She walked toward Mrs. Feldstein who gave her a big hug.

"We need to show we are behind you," she said quietly.

"I never doubted you," Maggie said honestly. "How can I help?"

"Just go to your office and get ready. We'll take care of everything."

Maggie nodded and turned to walk to her office. At the doorway she looked, back at her staff. This is the Timberview she knew, where one person's problem was everyone's problem. Things might work out all right yet.

The next couple of days were pretty routine. There were no more threats against the school. Maggie had everything in place for the meeting tonight. Hope was going to come in and work the evening. She would answer any questions concerning the office and office procedures. The custodians had everything clean and sparkling. Maggie had decided to have Hope call the bakery for some baked goods and they found an old coffee pot. They washed it out and used the coffee on. Maggie had been able to round up some National Honor Society students from the high school and they were set up in the library with cookies, milk, games, paper, crayons, markers and a TV with a VCR and a couple of movies they could show. Which is where the children would be. A couple of the boys said they would take some of the older kids out and start a baseball game. Maggie felt it would be great.

At six o'clock the staff started arriving they were going to have a brief meeting before the parents arrived. Maggie needed their full support to carry this off. All had arrived by six fifteen and Maggie started the meeting.

"First, I want to say, thank you," Maggie started. "I was overwhelmed when you took over and set things up for the meeting tonight. It's nice to know I have your support."

Mrs. Feldstein spoke up, "It's our school, too and we need to show the parents that their children will be safe."

"You are correct. It is the message I want the parents to receive tonight."

"Do you have an agenda?" Ida asked.

"No, I'm going to welcome all the parents and invite them to ask questions. I need to know their fears. If you don't mind, I'd like to let them walk through the building when we are done."

Brett was the first to say, "I'll be happy to open my room for parents."

The others all agreed.

"Well, since you all agree, I think we should drop in at the pizzeria afterward, my treat," replied Maggie.

Several people said they'd be there. Then the meeting broke up and the teachers went to get ready for parents. Coffee was put out, National Honor Society students were assigned to the library, VCR's were in place; paper, crayons, markers, cookies and milk were provided, and the teachers stood like a welcoming army as parents arrived. They directed parents to the library for their children and offered them coffee. Once everyone was seated, Maggie started the meeting.

"Good evening, I am Maggie Parsons, the new principal at Timberview Elementary. I am looking forward to an exciting year."

"I'll say," said a voice in the crowd.

Maggie ignored the voice and continued, "I want to thank each and every one of you for coming tonight. I know some of you have concerns about the safety of the school. I want to assure you, your children will be safe here. I thought I'd start by letting you ask questions."

A gentleman in the back stood. Maggie thought he looked familiar and then she recognized him as Glen Swift.

"Mr. Swift, please ask your question," she encouraged.

Glen blushed and said, "I understand they caught the person who vandalized the school."

"It's true they caught someone in the act."

Ashton stood then and said, "Then we should have nothing to fear."

Maggie smiled at her, "I believe, Mrs. Blythe you are correct."

"How do we know our kids will be safe?" asked a woman in the front row.

"I'm sorry I don't know your name," Maggie said, "but let me assure you all doors but the main one will be locked once the children are in class. No one will be able to sign your child out of the school unless their name is on the child's enrollment card. We will be asking for identification when someone other than a parent shows up to pick up your child. If your child is picked up after school, you will be picking them up from this room. All children will come through this room on their way to the buses. You may pick your child up here and follow out behind your child's class. This will prevent children from running through the parking lot. The local police are patrolling the area on a regular basis. Our staff has been trained on what to do in an emergency situation. We will have two lock down drills per year. They will not be announced and you will not be allowed to enter the building on those days.

"Why would you need to have lock down drills?" asked another gentleman.

"With schools becoming targets it is just a safety precaution. On those days the children will remain indoors at recess."

"Sounds like martial law. Why do I want my child to feel like he is in prison?" this from the lady sitting next to Glen.

"Your child should not feel like this is a prison, but he should feel safe coming here."

"Why didn't we have this with the old principal?" asked another woman.

"I'm sure I don't know."

"Does all this nonsense have to do with you being the principal?" the lady next to Glen asked.

"I'm not sure why my being principal has anything to do with this. The vandalism could have happened even if the old principal had not retired."

Glen piped up, "What Maggie says is true. There is no reason to believe any of this had to do with her. There was nothing here saying it was."

The woman next to him pulled on his arm to make him sit down.

Mrs. Feldstein spoke next, "I have been here almost thirty-five years. I have seen many of you grow up and watched our country change. When Mrs. Parsons was a young girl growing up in this town she ran errands for women who were shut-ins. She could have been off with her friends, but she took time out to show others she cared. She's the kind of person you want your children to look up to. None of this has anything to do with her. She has only recently moved back to town. There has been no time for anyone to form an opinion of what her capabilities as a principal will be. I think in all fairness to both Mrs. Parsons and your children, you should give her a chance to show you the good things which can and will happen here."

Several people said, "Here, here."

"Are there any other questions at this time?" Maggie asked. She saw no one stand and heard no response. "Since there don't seem to be any questions, the staff has agreed to open their rooms for you to walk through. I will remain here if you would like to ask your questions in private. On the way out be sure to take a pamphlet telling about our school, and how to reach me should you have questions in the future. Thank you again for coming tonight."

People moved to the door in an orderly fashion. Some people stopped to chat with neighbors. Others went on to their children's rooms.

One woman approached Maggie. She was a flashy blonde woman, in her tight jeans and too tight T-shirt with a flannel shirt over it, her hair was pulled back in a haphazard ponytail with tendrils falling at the sides. Maggie smiled as she approached.

"Miz Parsons, I'm Caylee Bright. My two boys will be startin' here on Monday. I think you are a right brave woman to stand up here and let people ask you questions. I want to thank you for bein' an example."

"Thank you very much. Maybe you will want to be part of our volunteer parent group," Maggie suggested.

"I don't think so. Most the ladies here in town just sees me as white trash. I do thank you kindly for askin'. I just want you to know my boys will be here."

"Thank you again for coming. I look forward to meeting your boys. Be sure and stop by their rooms."

"I'll do so. G'night now," she said as she walked away.

No one else approached Maggie. She walked to the door of the cafeteria and watched as parents and children made their way down the halls or out to their cars. She had a feeling this had been too easy. She would know better on Monday morning when the children arrived for school. She was disappointed none of the school board members had been present, nor was the superintendent, Mr. Whitehead. Their support would have helped the situation.

Maggie wondered, not for the first time, what she had walked into. Things were not exactly right here in Timberview. She felt as though she were standing on the brink of an abyss.

Half an hour after the meeting, Maggie and Hope walked through the school. All the classroom doors were locked and the teachers had gone to the pizzeria. They were almost back to the office when Hope said, "Maggie, what's going on?"

"What do you mean?"

"No one from administration was here and neither were school board members. It makes me wonder what is going on."

"I had those same thoughts myself. Maybe this is some kind of test they are putting the new principal through."

"I doubt it. Even if it was, you passed with flying colors. Every family showed up. Which is impressive."

"Thanks. Now let's finish locking up and go get some pizza."

"Great! I'll walk out with you."

The two women locked the building and walked to their cars. Three minutes later they joined the rest of the staff at the pizzeria. Several voiced opinions on how well the meeting went.

It was Ginny who commented on the lack of administrative support. "I even asked Mrs. Martin if she would be attending. She left me with the impression she would. I wonder what happened!"

"She's new on the board, someone most likely put pressure on her," Brett suggested.

After finishing up they all chipped in to pay for the pizza and headed for the parking lot. They said good night and each went their separate ways. Hope home to her husband and a quiet rest of the evening, the rest home with their own thoughts. Maggie to her mother's with grim thoughts and a nagging feeling this was not over.

Once home Maggie faced her mother. Estelle had a pot of tea on and wanted to hear all about the parent meeting. She had some crackers and cheese out, too.

"Maggie, tell me all about it," Estelle said as her daughter sat at the counter in the kitchen.

"Not much to tell," Maggie replied. "I pretty much told them what vandalism had occurred and then let them ask questions."

"Were any of the people rude?"

"No, in fact, it almost seemed to be too easy. No one was angry. No one was out of turn. It looks like most of the kids will be in school on Monday."

"What a relief. What did Mr. Whitehead have to say?"

"Nothing, he wasn't there."

"He knew about the meeting didn't he?"

"Yes, and so did all the school board members. None of them were there."

"Which seems a little odd."

"Yes, it does. Maybe they just felt I could handle it on my own."

"I'm sure they did, dear."

"Do you mind if I turn in? I'm really tired."

"No, dear, you run along off to bed."

"Good night, Mom, and thanks for the tea."

"Good night and you're welcome."

Maggie made her way to her bedroom. She put on her pajamas and climbed into bed. Then she took out a sheet of paper and began to make some notes.

Austin (Aussie) Howard had never left Timberview. He'd married and made his home here. His wife had recently died, no children. He'd worked as a custodian for the schools until last June.

Ashton (Blake) Blythe had just moved back to Timberview because of a divorce. She was enrolling a child in the school.

Glen Swift had moved back to Timberview two years ago when his father suddenly died. He had two boys enrolled in the school.

Matt Mitchell and his wife had just enrolled two children in the school. What brought him back to Timberview?

Where was Laura Gilbert these days? She would make up the threesome of girls. Aussie, Matt, and Glen had made up the three guys they'd hung out with. At least they had been the group until the day Aussie had been exposed as an imposter.

The girls had all dated all three of the boys at some point during high school, but they'd managed to remain friends, with the exception of Aussie.

Need to find out what brings Matt back. Need to see if I can learn where Laura is. What is our connection now?

Maggie put down her pad and pen. It was time for her to get some sleep. This was a puzzle she would turn over to Erika. It seemed like it might be all connected. She wondered where Laura was. They had kept in contact the first year of college, but after, it seemed the letters were fewer and farther between until they just stopped. She would ask her mother in the morning if she knew anything about Laura. Her mother had always liked her. Her mom might know what brought Matt and his family back to town too. Mom knew everything. Maggie smiled as she turned out the light.

She didn't realize she was screaming until her mother took her in her arms. It still took a few minutes for Maggie to pull herself out of the nightmare.

"I'm so sorry, Mom," she cried.

"It's alright," Estelle replied in the voice she'd used when Maggie was a child. She held her daughter a few minutes longer while the tremors left her body. Then she asked, "Would you like me to make some tea or cocoa?"

"No thanks. I should be able to go back to sleep. I'm so sorry I woke you."

"I'm okay. I just need to know you are."

"I'll be fine. I just need to get some sleep."

"All right, lie back."

Maggie lay back down in the bed and Estelle tucked the blankets around her. Then she quietly left the room. In the morning she was going to call her doctor. Something had to be done to prevent Maggie from having these awful nightmares.

Maggie's sleep was restless and she awoke several times. Something was nagging at the back of her mind and she couldn't put her finger on it. Something was just out of reach in her memory.

Maggie awoke very groggy on Friday morning, so she shortened her run and returned to find her mother making breakfast.

"Sorry I woke you last night, Mom," she said apologetically.

"You really need to see a doctor about these nightmares."

"I have seen a doctor. He prescribed sleeping pills and the nightmares got worse," Maggie replied. "I'm sure with time, they will go away." She turned and headed toward her room and a shower.

Estelle wondered why sleeping pills had been prescribed. Shouldn't Maggie be talking to someone? She'd call Dr. Gordon as soon as Maggie was gone.

Maggie ate a quick breakfast and drove to the school. There she found Hope already at her desk.

"Good morning," she said brightly, "no staff so far today. Abe Pentwater and I walked the building when I came in and there was nothing out of place."

"Thanks." Maggie proceeded to her office to see what the day held for her. Her calendar said she had an administrative meeting at 11 am. She'd better have something to report on the meeting last night. She picked up the phone to buzz Hope.

"Do we have any idea how many parents were here last night?" she asked when Hope picked up the phone.

"We sure do, I was just putting those numbers together for you. I'll bring it right in."

"Great!"

Hope brought Maggie the sheets the teachers had had in their rooms. They had asked each parent to sign in and put their child's name. Maggie was surprised there had been so many people in attendance. She had guessed about 200, but the signatures showed it was closer to 300. Which meant she had one hundred percent of her parents at the school. This was something to brag about. She had never been in a school which had this kind of turn out for a parent meeting. She hoped she could keep it going all year.

Maggie spent the next hour typing a report using the data Hope had given her and notes Hope had taken during the meeting. When she was finished she asked Hope to proof read it then made copies to take with her to the meeting.

Maggie told Hope to look for her after one o'clock as she did not know how long the administration meeting would be and she would be stopping to get lunch before coming back. Then she headed confidently out to her car and to the meeting ahead.

The meeting turned out to be more of an execution than a meeting. Maggie presented everyone with her report at the beginning of the meeting.

"Of course you had a one hundred percent turn out, people want to know their kids are safe," Mr. Whitehead said disgustedly his rotund body shaking with the effort. "Do you really think they would have come otherwise?"

Mr. Allenby, the high school principal said, "It's nice to know parents will come out for safety. Too, bad you couldn't have had something positive to celebrate."

"How do you intend to deal with other situations which will arise from this mess?"

"I don't expect there to be any other situations related to this," Maggie said firmly. "This was an isolated incident of vandalism. I doubt it will be repeated."

"I should hope not," Ms. Wells chimed in. She was the middle school principal, a pencil thin woman with half glasses she perched on the end of her nose and looked over when she talked to you.

Maggie turned to Mr. Albin Thomas, assistant high school principal and athletic director and asked, "Would you like to jump in here and make any comments?"

To which Mr. Thomas replied, "I don't feel any more comments are necessary."

Mr. Whitehead agreed and dismissed everyone except for Maggie. When the others were gone he said, "Mrs. Parsons, I am not pleased with how things are working out. I am hereby putting you on notice if this type of thing continues, we will not renew your contract at the end of your second year. Am I understood?"

"You certainly are, however I might point out to you bear some responsibility for what has happened. You fired Mr. Howard last spring. You were also absent at the meeting last night, so none of those issues were addressed. I will refer parents to you for comment." Maggie picked up her briefcase and left the room.

She stopped for a salad at the Diner and then returned to the school.

Hope saw the look in her eye and decided it would be best not to ask how the meeting went. Instead she smiled and said, "These just came for you."

Maggie looked at the red roses and smiled. She wondered who they were from. She looked at the card and frowned. It read:

> *Roses are red*
> *Violets are blue*
> *I remember high school*
> *Do you?*

"What? Who?" Maggie looked at Hope with a puzzled expression.

"I thought it was some kind of code," Hope said expectantly.

"I have no idea who sent these. Do you know who delivered them?"

"Only florist in town is Flowerama."

"Can you get them on the phone for me?"

"Sure," Hope said as Maggie walked into her office. Hope dialed the number and waited for Mae Townsend to pick up. When she did Hope said, "Mae, please hold for Mrs. Parsons."

"Mrs. Parsons," Maggie said into the phone.

"Mrs. Parsons, this is Betty Townsend at Flowerama. Did your flowers arrive?"

"They did. Do you know who they are from?" Maggie asked sharply.

"No, the money was wired in with the directions and the note for the card was with them."

"Thank you very much, so sorry to have bothered you."

"Any time, I hope everything is all right."

Maggie did not wait to say good-bye she hung up and called Erika Estwick.

22

"This is E and E Investigations, how may I help you?"

"May I speak to Erika Estwick, please?"

"I'm sorry Ms. Estwick is out of the office today. May I take a message?"

"Yes, please ask her to call Maggie Parsons as soon as she can."

"May I tell her what it's regarding?"

"Tell her I received some suspicious flowers."

"It's flowers as in the plant?"

"Yes." Maggie was getting more frustrated by the minute.

"Does she have your number?"

"I believe so; my home number is 218-645-4595."

"I'll give her your message when she checks in."

"Thank you." Maggie hung up the phone and wished not for the first time this day was over.

At the end of the day Maggie made the walkthrough of the building alone. When she got back to the office Hope was waiting for her.

"You could have gone home," Maggie said.

"Yep, I could have. I just didn't want you alone in the building."

"Thanks, but it wasn't necessary."

"I know, but it's what friends do for each other."

The two women walked to their cars. As she was getting into her car Hope said, "Things will be okay on Monday when the kids are here."

"I hope so. You have a good week-end."

"You, too," Hope called as she drove away.

Maggie looked back at the school. Was it possible she had stumbled into something sinister in her old home town? Things were not what they seemed in Timberview. Not what they seemed at all. With that thought, she got into her car and drove home.

M aggie came quietly into the house. Her mom was not in the kitchen. Which seemed odd, but then most things did these days. Maggie made her way to her room, took off her clothes, put on a robe and went to take a shower. After her shower she found her mother in the kitchen.

"How was your day?" Estelle asked.

"Rather routine for a change," Maggie replied. "Mom, can I ask you something?"

"You can ask me whatever you'd like."

"It's two questions actually. Do you know what brought Matt Mitchell back to town? Have you ever heard what happened to Laura Gilbert?"

Estelle didn't miss a beat although her heart fluttered in her chest. "Matt was laid off from his job and his dad wants to retire, so Matt came home to run the business."

"And what about Laura do you know where she is?" Maggie asked expectantly.

"Well, it's a long story and I know some of it."

"I'm waiting to hear. I haven't heard from Laura since my sophomore year of college."

"In the early part of your sophomore year, Ashton's mother and I learned Laura was pregnant. It wouldn't have been so bad, but she was going to raise the baby alone. She wouldn't tell anyone who the father was. So, we wrote to her, each of us sending some money and told her not to contact you and Ashton again. We told her, you no longer wanted to associate with her." Estelle hung her head.

"Oh, Mother, you didn't!" Maggie cried astounded by her mother's audacity.

"I'm afraid to say we did," she replied. "I cannot tell you how ashamed I am now for what I have done. Laura was like a daughter. I kept my guilt at bay by sending her more money. I think I sent about a thousand dollars in all."

"What makes you think *that* was right? Laura was my friend, the sister I never had and when she needed me most you told her to get lost. Do you have any idea where she is now?"

"I haven't heard a word since we sent the first letter. I'm sorry, Maggie." Estelle continued to make dinner. "While I'm at it I might as well tell you I called Dr. Gordon and he is coming by tonight to prescribe you some sleeping pills. These nightmares cannot go on. Not if you want to do a good job."

"Let me guess, word is out I have been put on notice if there are anymore incidents at the school and I will be dismissed," said Maggie sarcastically.

"Oh, Maggie, no!" her mother exclaimed.

"Yes, that was the last part of my meeting with the superintendent today. I am very frustrated being blamed for this break in."

"I know you are, dear," Estelle said soothingly. "Just give it some time and things will fall into a routine."

"I'd like to believe it," Maggie said with a sigh. "In the meantime, I have a few more questions about some of my classmates."

I'll try to answer them."

"Well, it seems a bit odd to me the entire crowd I hung around with has recently come back to Timberview. Take Glen Swift for example, didn't you tell me he came back to help out his mom after his dad died?"

"Yes, Will died suddenly. The next thing we knew, Glen had moved his family back here and taken over his father's lumber mill. Seems it was a good thing as he had been out of work for about three months when Will died."

Estelle moved the food from the pan to plates and brought them to the counter. She sat down and said, "Funny you should ask we were just talking about it at lunch today. It seems he was about to lose his job and his dad decided to retire. Matt came home to run the hardware."

"What an odd coincidence," Maggie commented. Then she lifted a fork full of food to her mouth. They sat in quiet companionship through the rest of the meal. Each lost in her own thoughts.

When they were done, Maggie offered to do the dishes. Estelle took her coffee to the living room and sat in her chair to read the paper. Maggie was just finishing the dishes when Dr. Gordon arrived. He was tall with snow white hair and a trim physic, what some would call distinguished.

Estelle ushered him into the living room along with Maggie. Once they were all seated she began, "Tell Dr. Gordon about your nightmares, Maggie."

Maggie began to fidget.

"Estelle, why don't you bring us some coffee, tea for Maggie," Dr. Gordon said. He looked at Estelle and continued, "Maggie might need some privacy."

Estelle was not pleased at being dismissed in her own home, but she stood and marched from the room with as much dignity as she could muster.

Maggie let out the breath she had not been aware she was holding. "Thank you, Dr. Gordon," she began, "I don't know what Mom has told you, but since the accident I have night-mares. The doctor in Davenport prescribed sleeping pills, but the nightmares seemed to get worse."

"I don't think sleeping pills is the answer, Maggie," said Dr. Gordon. "Have you tried anti-depressants?"

"Aren't those for people who are depressed?"

"Grief is a form of depression. I thought we might try a low dose of an anti-depressant. I also think you need to go to grief counseling." He held up his hand before Maggie could object. "Grief counseling isn't like being crazy, it helps you to understand what you are going through and it allows you to go through it."

"If I can have peaceful sleep, I'm willing to try," Maggie said.

"Good, I'll write a prescription. You should get it filled in the morning. I did bring a dose for tonight." He handed Maggie a pill in a sealed one dose container. Then he turned toward the kitchen and said, "It's okay, Estelle, you can come back now."

He and Maggie shared a knowing smile as Estelle walked back into the living room with three steaming mugs, cream and sugar on a tray. She set the tray on the coffee table and each one took a cup.

"I assume you have taken care of Maggie's problem," Estelle said, "however I don't know what could have been so secret I couldn't be here to hear it."

"Doctor-patient confidentiality," Dr. Gordon replied, "besides Maggie is an adult and entitled to her privacy; even in your house."

Estelle made a guttural sound in her throat.

Maggie stood and held her hand out to the doctor, "Thank you Dr. Gordon. You can have your secretary call mine with times for the meetings." She turned to her mother and said, "Good night." Then she walked to her bedroom.

Estelle seethed. "That was uncalled for, James. I have every right to know what is going on with my daughter."

"Not under the law, Stell. I wanted her to feel at ease talking to me and wasn't going to happen with you in the room. It's never been easy with you and Maggie. Give her some space, she'll tell you in her own time."

Estelle was not appeased, but nodded her head in agreement as she sipped her coffee.

Dr. Gordon finished his coffee and Estelle walked him to the door. He leaned down to brush her cheek with a kiss. "You need to tell her about us, Stell, before some town gossip does."

"I will when the time is right." She wrapped her arms around him and gave him a full-mouth kiss. Then she watched him walk to his car and drive away.

This was one more reason Maggie needed a good night's sleep and a place of her own. Estelle was ready to get on with her own life.

Maggie stretched like a satisfied cat and opened her eyes to the morning sunlight filtering through her curtains. She felt rested for the first time since the accident. She would have to thank Dr. Gordon for whatever it was he'd given her.

As she dressed for her morning run, she could smell the coffee her mother was brewing. Then she glanced at the clock and gasped. She hadn't slept until nine since she was a teen. Quickly she headed for the kitchen.

On the counter was a note from her mother. It said;

> Maggie,
>
> I let you sleep. The phones are turned off. Breakfast is warming in the oven. I've gone to the market.
>
> Love,
> Mother

Maggie flipped the switch to turn on the kitchen phone and headed out the back door for her run. Unlike most mornings, Maggie found herself greeted by friends and neighbors along the way. She arrived home in time to help her mother carry in the groceries. Once the groceries were in the house Maggie went to take a shower.

When she returned to the kitchen, her mother had the groceries put away, poured herself a cup of coffee, was boiling water for Maggie's tea, and had set breakfast on the counter.

"Mmm," Maggie said as the aroma from the quiche wafted toward her, "I love quiche."

"It was no trouble. I don't often make it when I'm alone," Estelle said.

"Thanks, Mom," Maggie said between bites.

"Erika Estwick called while you were in the shower," Estelle said softly.

Maggie looked curiously at her mother, "What did she say?"

"She'll be here at two, so she can bring you up to date on what she's learned."

"Okay," Maggie replied hesitantly, "Is there a problem?"

Estelle studied her coffee then said, "It's just I have a book club luncheon meeting at one. I could call and give my regrets."

"It's not necessary," replied Maggie. "You and I can talk about the findings or lack of them when you get back."

Estelle sighed and said, "If you're sure…"

Maggie walked around the counter and gave her a hug. "Thanks for caring, but I need to do this by myself."

Estelle patted Maggie's hand and took her cup of coffee to the living room to finish the book for the meeting. Maggie finished her breakfast and did the dishes. She didn't interrupt her mother as she made her way to her bedroom.

Maggie took out her notebook. She had a lot of questions for Erika. She hoped Erika had some answers for her. She wanted to know why her family had died a horrible death.

Maggie had a quick lunch and had finished the dishes, put them away, changed into a baby blue linen suit, and had water on for tea by the time Erika arrived. She offered Erika a cup of tea and the two of them went to the living room. Erika, dressed in a peach suit, seated herself on the sofa and Maggie sat in her father's chair.

"I'd like to get right down to business," Erika began. "I've done a thorough investigation of your husband's business and his business partners. I've also turned some of the information I found over to the district attorney. Arrests are being made today."

Maggie stifled a gasp.

"I learned your husband's two partners have been swindling you and others out of their investments. Which is something to be handled by the courts," Erika stated.

Maggie started to ask, "When did they..."

"Please let me finish," Erika interrupted, "I know you are going to have a lot of questions. Let me tell you what I know."

Maggie nodded and sank back into the old chair taking comfort from the familiar.

"It seems your husband started asking questions about six months ago. He had hired an outside accountant to look at the books. His two partners were afraid of being exposed so they got together and hired someone to kill him."

"Oh, my God, they killed my children!" Maggie couldn't help from saying.

"It seems the children were just in the wrong place," Erika continued. "It's going to get them conspiracy to commit murder charges along with three counts of murder. They will also face embezzlement charges. You will be able to file for wrongful death and collect damages." Erika stopped and looked at Maggie's white face.

"I know this is not what you were hoping to hear," she said quietly, "I'm truly sorry, Maggie. Now let me get you some more tea and I'll answer your questions."

Erika went to the kitchen with Maggie's cup. While making the tea she looked in the cupboards until she found what she was looking for. She added a generous serving of whiskey to the tea and returned to the living room.

Maggie was numb. She could hardly believe Ben's partners were stealing from the company, much less they planned his murder; the same murder which ultimately took the lives of her children. She picked up the tea Erika set on the coffee table, took a swallow, and began coughing.

"I'm sorry. I thought you could use some of my grandma's strength recipe," Erika said with a slight grin.

Maggie recovered from her coughing spell to say, "You were right."

"Good, now what questions do you want to ask?"

Maggie reached for her notebook, "First, how long had this been going on?"

"I gather it had only been going on in the last year. It was not something they started out doing. Both men were living way beyond their means. At first they were taking from clients, then they tapped into the account Ben had for the two of you. They did not get into the account for the children."

"Ben found out about it?"

"I believe so. From things I've learned the three of them had a heated discussion. They wanted Ben to join them."

"He would never have done that."

Erika looked at her and said, "Exactly, so he had to be eliminated before he could expose them."

"What else have you learned?" Maggie asked. She had a feeling she was not going to like what she heard.

"One of the partners has a mistress," Erika began.

"Does it make a difference?" Maggie prompted.

"Her name is Laura Gilbert," Erika continued.

Again Maggie stifled a gasp, and said, "Go on, I need to hear what you know."

"Laura has become quite a businesswoman in her own right. She is the owner of Gilbert Antiques Gallery and Gifts. She has been the mistress to several powerful gentlemen. Her daughter, Ashton Margaret, attends a private college somewhere out east."

"Ashton Margaret?" said a startled Maggie.

"Why does the name shock you?"

"We were all friends in high school; Laura, Ashton, and I. I am Margaret."

Erika nodded, "It might make a difference."

"How could it make a difference? If she has been with all these powerful men, how did she end up with one of Ben's business partners?"

"I'm not sure yet. I'm still working on how she became mixed up with one of Ben's partners. Do you have the list of people you said you went around with in high school?"

Maggie nodded and reached for her notebook again. She found the page she'd started and handed it to Erika.

"These people aren't involved are they?"

"No, believe it or not I think they are victims, just like you." Erika looked at the list. "I need to do some more digging can we meet sometime next week?"

"It will have to be in the evening as school starts on Monday," Maggie replied.

"I've made a written copy of what I just told you. I want you to look it over during the week and see if you have any more questions. I have included a contract in the packet. I am still trying to trace your flowers, but I believe they probably came from Laura Gilbert."

Maggie was too stunned to take in anymore. She walked Erika to her car and said she'd call her on Wednesday to set up another meeting. Then she walked back to the living room to read through the papers.

Maggie knew her mother would want to hear everything when she returned. So, she made a list of things she could refer to. It hardly seemed possible Ben's partners had killed her family. She knew these men and their wives. Three families destroyed for money. Maggie just shook her head in disbelief.

Then she began to wonder how Laura Gilbert fit into all of this. Laura had a daughter in college, she'd named after Ashton and herself. She was the owner of an antiques store and art gallery. She was considered a good business woman. What was her role if any in all of this? Who was she having an affair with? How long had the affair been going on? Why would she send me flowers? These were questions Maggie wrote down to ask Erika about next week. Surely some of this could be explained. Maybe it was just a coincidence Laura was involved with one of Ben's partners. Deep in her heart Maggie knew it was not, but she had to believe Laura was not involved. If she didn't, she would have to start asking why? How?

The first thing she wanted to know from her mother is whether or not Mr. and Mrs. Gilbert still lived in Timberview. Maybe she should visit them. She'd spent as many hours there as she had at Ashton's when they were growing up.

Maggie made herself another cup of tea laced with a generous portion of whiskey. This was just too much to take in.

Estelle found Maggie sleeping in her father's chair, papers and notes were scattered all over the floor. She picked up the tea cup had fallen from Maggie's hand, glad to see she had finished her tea before letting go. Estelle sniffed, the cup smelled odd. Whiskey, in the middle of the day! Maggie didn't even drink whiskey.

After taking the cup into the kitchen, Estelle went back into the living room. She needed to know what Maggie had learned and if it was why she'd drunk enough to make her sleep.

"Maggie," she said quietly, "it's Mom. You need to wake up now."

Maggie awoke groggily. "Mom, what time is it?"

"Almost time to start dinner. How did your meeting with Ms. Estwick go?"

As Maggie became more alert she started looking for the papers she had dropped. "It was not pleasant. Give me a minute and I will tell you about it. I made notes."

Estelle walked to her ladder back chair and sat. She knew this was not the time to scold. She'd wait until she heard what Maggie had found out, and then she'd scold.

Maggie quickly pulled herself together. She wondered if maybe she should make some tea and whiskey for her mother, then decided against it.

"First I want you to let me tell you everything Erika said. Then you can ask questions. I might be able to answer some and there might be some I want answers to as well," Maggie said calmly.

"It's fine, dear," Estelle answered dreading what she would hear.

"Ok, this is what I now know; Ben had found some discrepancies in our accounts. He took them to an outside accountant and learned his partners were skimming from some of the accounts. They had a heated discussion which led to the partners hiring someone to kill Ben. The fact the children were with him didn't matter to the killer," Maggie paused here to take a breath.

"You mean my grandchildren were murdered?"

Maggie nodded. "It also seems one of the partners is having an affair. His mistress is Laura Gilbert. Laura has a daughter in college out east whose name is Ashton Margaret."

Estelle gasped, and then said, "What does Laura have to do with the death of Ben and the children?"

"I don't know yet. Do Mr. and Mrs. Gilbert still live here?"

"Heavens, no, Mr. Gilbert had a stroke shortly after Laura announced she was pregnant and keeping the child. He went into a nursing home and died about six months later. Mrs. Gilbert sold the house and moved away."

"I'm sorry I didn't know."

"Erika seems to think some of my classmates might be victims too. I'm not sure how and she is looking into it."

"What are the police going to do with this information?"

"Jack Westin and Bill Scott have been arrested and charged with embezzlement, conspiracy to commit murder and three counts of murder," Maggie said with a calmness she didn't feel.

"It's time my family had justice," Estelle said fiercely.

"You realize Adam and Alyssa were murdered just because they were with Ben?"

"Yes, they were killed before they had a chance to experience life. I am so sorry."

"I am too, Mom. I had them for ten wonderful years. I think the nightmares come as much from me imagining the accident as from me trying to save them and failing."

"Maybe with closure you can start healing."

"Maybe and one way is to talk to the realtor in Davenport. I think I'll call him tomorrow."

Estelle went to Maggie and gave her a hug. She was surprised when Maggie hugged her back and began to sob. She held her daughter until her tears subsided.

Since it was Saturday, more people seemed to be out when Maggie went for her morning run. She waved a greeting to those she passed. At home she showered and dressed, then headed for the kitchen. Her mother was sitting at the table with a cup of coffee reading the morning paper.

"So, Mom," Maggie said, "what big plans to you have for today?"

"I have a lunch meeting with some friends, and then I will go to the market before coming home," Estelle answered distractedly.

"Ok, I'm going to call the realtor from Davenport. I may go over there later."

Estelle looked up. "Should you take Martin with you?"

"No, I need to do this on my own."

"Call if you need anything."

"I will," Maggie said as she popped two slices of bread in the toaster and began looking for the peanut butter and some jam.

By the time Maggie had finished her breakfast and washed the dishes, her mother had disappeared. She didn't give it much thought as she went to her room to find the letter from the realtor. She placed the call from her room.

"Real One Real Estate, how may I help you?" said the young woman answering the phone.

"May I speak with Mr. Baker please?" Maggie asked.

"May I tell him who's calling?"

"It's Mrs. Parsons, calling about a letter he sent."

"One moment please."

Maggie was barely on hold when the phone was picked up.

"Robert Baker here, Mrs. Parsons."

"Do you still have a buyer for my home?"

"I believe I do. How soon would you be ready to sell?"

"It would depend on the offer, Mr. Baker."

"I believe it might bring you about $150,000," he said smugly.

"I don't think we can do business then," Maggie replied. "Your offer is at least $100,000 below the market value. Thank you for your time." Maggie hung up the phone.

She decided it was time to go to the house. She needed to pack up the things still there and get it ready for sale. She heard the phone ring as she closed the back door. The answering machine could pick it up.

Maggie stopped to get gas on her way out of town. The drive to Davenport would take a good two hours. She picked up a bottle of water and a candy bar to keep her company.

The drive seemed to fly by and Maggie found herself pulling into her driveway. The lawn company had kept the lawn mowed and the weeds pulled in the flower beds. It looked welcoming. She stepped out of the car and headed for the back door. She didn't want to talk to neighbors at the moment.

As she closed the door and turned to the kitchen she half expected the twins to come running toward her telling her about their day. She fought back tears. Someone had cleaned the kitchen after the funeral dinner. It was spotless.

Maggie left the kitchen and walked slowly through the rooms downstairs. Everywhere there were reminders of her family. As she headed up the stairs she stopped fighting the tears.

Her first stop was Adam's room. It was way too neat. There should have been clothes, shoes, and baseball cards strewn about the room. His desk was orderly, so unlike her energetic son. He'd have had books and papers scattered all over it. The thought made Maggie smile.

Alyssa's room too was neat, but it always had been. Adam often called her a neat freak. He was smart enough to hire her to help him get his room cleaned up when he wanted something. Alyssa would have been the money maker. On the shelf above her bed was her coin bank. She'd been saving for a computer. With a sigh, Maggie left the room and headed toward her own.

Her room the one she had shared with Ben for thirteen years. The one she had retreated to when tragedy struck. It was just an empty room now except for the furniture. There was no scent of Ben in the room. She could not feel him there.

She walked down the stairs and took out her cell phone. The first call she made was to Madeline Welch a long time friend and real estate agent.

"Hello," said the young voice on the other end.

"May I speak to Mrs. Welch please?" Maggie asked.

"Sure." Maggie heard the phone clunk as it was dropped on a counter, then "Mom, it's for you."

"This is Maddy Welsh."

"Maddy it's Maggie Parsons."

"Maggie, how are you? Where are you?"

"I'm here in Davenport. I'm at the house actually. I was wondering if you'd list it for me."

"Are you sure you want to do this?"

"Yes, I'm sure."

"Then give me about fifteen minutes and I'll be there."

"I'll see if I can find some tea to put on."

"Okay, bye."

Maggie disconnected and started looking through the cupboards. There were tea bags in the canister. She put water in the kettle and set it on to boil. Then she took down two coffee mugs. She rummaged around some more and found some instant coffee creamer and an unopened box of sugar packets. These were not things she usually had in the cupboard, but they would do.

It took less than ten minutes for Maddy to pull into the driveway. She stepped out of her car looking like a cover model and not like a real estate agent. Her blond hair cut fashionably short giving her an elfin look. She was dressed in a white linen suit with the skirt above her knees and white linen sandals. Maggie went out to meet her with a cup of tea in her hand. Maddy took the cup and set it on the roof of her car. Then she enveloped Maggie in a hug.

"How are you really?" she asked as she stepped back and retrieved the cup of tea.

"I'm doing ok," Maggie answered honestly. "I've had to accept Ben and the kids are not coming back and I need to move on."

"I'm so sorry."

"I know. It was very hard when I learned they had been killed on purpose. I think it's when I decided I needed closure. Selling the house will give me that. It's time I move on."

"Murdered! You can't mean it, Maggie," Maddy exclaimed. "Surely a drunk driver does not necessarily make it murder."

"Come inside, Maddy," Maggie said, "there are some things you don't know.

The two women walked into the house and Maggie told Maddy what she had learned from Erika Estwick. They then toured the house and Maddy took measurements and photos as they went.

"I think we can easily list this at $250,000," Maddy said as they went back downstairs. "Are you going to store the furniture?"

"Not just yet," Maggie replied, "I am going to take some personal things with me and I will be bringing Marty back to help me take some others. I thought the house might sell better if there was some furniture in it."

"You are right. We can stage it so buyers will love it."

"Good. What papers do I need to sign?"

"Just a couple and I have a sign in my car if you want me to put it out now."

"Can you wait on the sign until I drive away?"

"Not a problem, Maggie."

Maggie signed the papers which needed to be signed for Maddy to list the property. She handed a set of keys over to Maddy, picked up a few things she had put in a basket she found in a closet and headed for her car. As she drove away she saw Maddy putting the for sale sign in her yard.

She sighed. That part of her life was over. It was time to move on. For now, she would call her mother's house home while she looked for a small place for herself.

The busses rolled in carrying their precious cargo and Maggie stood on the side walk to greet the children. She could feel their excitement as they went into the building. She'd felt it many times herself. A new year always brought excitement to the classroom. Now she was in charge of the whole building. Maggie walked in behind the last of the children.

Hope motioned to her as she walked by the office window. She went in to see what it was.

"Sorry, Maggie," Hope said as she pointed to the phone, "Mr. Whitehead."

"I'll take it in my office," Maggie said and continued walking. The phone rang and she picked it up.

"This is Mrs. Parsons. How may I help you?"

"Mrs. Parsons, I thought I'd made it clear to you, I wanted no more scandal," Whitehead nearly shouted into the phone.

"I have no idea what you are talking about," Maggie asked calmly.

"I just read the morning paper it says you have hired a private investigator to look into the break in at the school. We have a police force to handle things of this nature."

"I'm sorry, Mr. Whitehead, but the newspaper is mistaken in its facts. I did hire a private investigator, but it was to look into the accident which killed my husband and children."

"Well, we'll just see about that!" Whitehead said and slammed down the phone.

Maggie shook her head. Small town gossip was going to put her out of a job before she ever got started. While she was here she would do her very best. Which meant stopping in each classroom this morning to say 'hello' to the students.

Maggie stopped only long enough to tell Hope her plan then left the office for the pre-k classroom.

Once Maggie had stopped in all the classes, she returned to the office.

"Any new crisis?" she asked Hope as she walked in.

"Nothing we can't handle," Hope replied with a smile.

Maggie went to her office to review the plan she and Hope had made for the day. Maggie was to do some paperwork until lunch time. When she would be in the lunch room. She hoped to spend some time with each lunch group. The day went smoothly until after lunch.

Abigail Marsh, one of the playground aides, came breathlessly into the office at the end of recess. "Brandon Mitchell and Greg Swift are missing!"

"What do you mean they're missing?" Hope asked quietly.

"They didn't come in from recess with the rest of their class. No one can find them," Abigail replied.

Maggie came from her office to see what was going on.

"I'm so sorry, Mrs. Parsons," Abigail said through tears, "I didn't see anyone come onto the playground, but the boys are gone."

Calmly Maggie looked from Hope to Abigail then she asked, "What boys are gone where?"

"Evidently Brandon Mitchell and Greg Swift did not come in from recess with the rest of their class," Hope replied.

"I want every adult who is not a teacher in this office now," Maggie said as she went back into her office.

In no time the custodian, kitchen help, librarian, and the three playground aides were in the office.

"This is the plan. Hope, I want you to ask all teachers to keep their students in their rooms until further notice. We are going to divide into groups. We are each taking a level, I want every nook and cranny in this building covered. We will meet back here in no longer than ten minutes. She handed a walkie-talkie to one member of each group. If you find the boys, notify us on these. Are there any questions?"

No one said a word each group started off through the building. In ten minutes they were back in the office, without the boys.

"Put us in lockdown," she said as she picked up the phone and dialed Sheriff Norton.

"Sheriff's office."

"This is Maggie Parsons at the elementary. I have two missing boys. I need Sheriff Norton here immediately. I have assembled all available adults to begin a search of the playground area, he will find me there."

"I'll tell him, Mrs. Parsons."

Maggie hung up the phone grabbed a handful of PE whistles and headed out. She let Hope know Sheriff Norton should be sent out to the playground when he arrived. No one else was to enter the building.

Once on the playground Maggie looked at the people there and said, "We do not know what the situation is. What we do know is two little boys, Brandon Mitchell and Greg Swift did not come back in from recess. Pair up; I will give each pair a whistle, and you still have your walkie-talkies. Use them only if you find them. Abigail, please wait here for Sheriff Norton, he will want to take a statement. Do you remember the last time you saw the boys?"

Abigail nodded, and then said, "I saw them out near the woods."

"Thank you. Ok, everyone spread out an arms length apart and let's start looking."

As the group set out, Maggie could hear the sirens in the distance. She was frightened the boys could be hurt or worse and it would be her fault. She kept the tension at bay by focusing on where she was going. There was a break in the school yard fence. It needed to be mended.

Sheriff Norton caught up with her just as she was about to enter the woods. "Mrs. Parsons," he called.

Maggie turned briefly to acknowledge him. Her face was white.

He came along side her and said quietly, "You are doing fine. It will be okay."

"Easy for you to say, I just want the boys found."

"You are doing everything by the book. We'll find them. One day we will even laugh about this."

"Not anytime soon," Maggie assured him.

They were about fifty feet into the woods, when Maggie heard a whimper. "Did you hear that?" she asked.

They stopped to listen. Then Sheriff Norton looked up. Sitting twenty feet up in a tree were two terrified little boys.

Maggie lifted her walkie-talkie and said, "We have them. They are in a tree." She heard the cheer as soon as she stopped talking. Then she heard everyone running through the woods to where they were.

Sheriff Norton said to the boys, "Can you make it down?"

Brandon Mitchell sniffed and said, "No, I think I broke my arm."

Greg Swift said, "I can come down now, but I couldn't leave Brandon up here alone."

"Okay, Greg, you climb down. Brandon, don't move I'll be up as soon as Greg is down."

Greg was down from the tree in no time. He walked to Maggie with his head down. "I'm sorry, Mrs. Parsons, it was my idea to climb the tree."

Maggie hugged the boy and said, "We'll figure it out later, Greg, right now I'm glad you are okay."

Abby Marsh arrived breathless and scooped Greg into her arms. "You had me so frightened young man." Tears of joy ran down her face as she inspected him and found him to be okay. "Where is Brandon?"

Greg pointed to the tree where Sheriff Norton was swiftly climbing the branches.

"Oh, my goodness!" Abby exclaimed. "You just hang on there Brandon."

Brandon just nodded as he watched Sheriff Norton coming toward him.

"Okay, Brandon, tell me which arm hurts," the Sheriff said when he was close enough to reach the child safely. He leaned into a branch to brace himself as he removed his belt.

"This one," Brandon said indicating his left arm. "I tried to climb down, but I slipped. That's when Greg came back up to stay with me. Please don't be mad at him."

"I'm not mad. It was a good thing for him to stay with you. Now I'm going to move in closer and put my belt around your arm so it is tight to your body."

The Sheriff moved in and placed his belt around Brandon to stabilize his arm. Then he lifted the child into his own arms and said, "Brandon, I need you to put your good arm around me and wrap your legs around my waist."

Brandon did as he was told and the two made it down the tree.

Once they were safely on the ground, Maggie let out the breath she had been holding. She was glad the boys were unhurt, but knew there would be fallout from this. Sheriff Norton carried Brandon back to the school.

Maggie gave Hope the all clear and classes went back to normal. She called both families and asked them to come to the school.

She then went to her office where she had sent Sheriff Norton. She found him standing looking out the window, a cup of tea in his hand.

"I hope you don't mind, I helped myself to the tea," he said without emotion.

"Not at all, it's the least I can do. Thank you for your assistance today."

"I think we know where those two men escaped to the day you called. The fence was deliberately cut and it was cut recently."

"I'll get maintenance on the repairs right away."

"No, please let me send out a team and see if we can get any fingerprints first."

Maggie hesitated. "Okay, but I need to know my children will be safe. I cannot have them wandering off into the woods, just because the fence is open."

"I'll make a call and have someone out here right away," the Sheriff offered. "Then you can have them fix the fence tomorrow."

"That will be fine."

Hope walked in then to let Maggie know Mr. Mitchell had arrived and Mr. Swift was on his way. Maggie thanked her and followed her to the outer office. Sheriff Norton came behind them.

"Matt, it's good to see you," Maggie began.

"I'm so sorry he caused you trouble."

"Mr. Mitchell," the Sheriff said, "I put my belt around him to stabilize his arm. I think it might be broken."

"Thanks, Sheriff, we'll head right for the hospital."

Maggie saw them signed out and leaving the building as Glen Swift came up the walk.

"Maggie, what has he done?" Glen asked.

"He frightened ten years off my life, but he did the right thing, Glen."

Greg looked at his dad and said, "I wanted to climb a tree and Brandon went ahead of me, but he got scared coming down. Then he fell and broke his arm. I stayed with him in the tree, Dad."

Glen looked from Greg to Maggie. "Tell me he didn't."

"That's pretty much it in a nutshell," Maggie answered. "When we couldn't find the boys in the building we went looking. I called the Sheriff to be on the safe side. I must admit it's made for a pretty exciting first day."

"A little too exciting, I'd say." Glen looked at his son, "I won't be letting you off as easy as Mrs. Parsons. You had a lot of people worried about you."

Maggie saw the first tear begin to trickle down Greg's cheek and said, "We'll start over again tomorrow."

Glen signed Greg out and took him home. Maggie was sure Greg had not heard the end of this. She was also sure she would hear more about this as soon as Mr. Whitehead learned of it. With a deep sigh she looked at the Sheriff and said, "If there's nothing more Sheriff, I need to make a couple more phone calls."

"No, I've got someone coming and I'll show them where to look. Then I'll be out of here."

"Thank you," Maggie said and turned toward her office. Her first call would be to Mr. Whitehead.

In her office she dialed the extension to Mr. Whitehead's office. After the call this morning, she was sure this would be her last day as the principal.

"Mr. Whitehead," he said shortly when he answered the phone.

"This is Maggie Parsons," she replied calmly.

"What can I do for you Mrs. Parsons?"

"I'm calling to report we had an incident today. Brandon Mitchell and Greg Swift did not come in from recess. We searched the building, then called the Sheriff, and went to the playground to begin a search. The boys were located off school property; they had gone through the fence where someone had cut it. They were both in a tree, Brandon with a broken arm and Greg unhurt. The Sheriff brought Brandon down and his father has taken him to the emergency room. Mr. Swift came and took Greg home." She got it all out then held her breath.

"Thank you for your report," Mr. Whitehead said. "I understand you kept your cool and things were handled very well. If there's nothing else I have work to do."

"Uh, no," Maggie stuttered. As she hung up the phone, she let out the breath she'd been holding and wondered what brought the change in Mr. Whitehead. Where was the man who had been ranting earlier this morning? What about his threat a scandal would get her fired? Something strange was going on.

The rest of the day was incident free and Maggie was there to see the children safely on the busses. When she entered the office the entire staff was there.

"Way to go!" they all cheered.

Maggie blushed. "I have done nothing anyone else wouldn't have done. Go home and enjoy your evening."

The group dispersed. Hope and Maggie closed up the office and went their separate ways toward home.

Maggie drove slowly home. She wondered if every day was going to bring something like this. She was still puzzled over Mr. Whitehead's reaction and his ranting earlier in the day.

"Hi, Mom," she called as she came in the back door.

"Tell me all about it," Estelle said breathlessly.

Maggie sat down at on one of the stools at the counter. "It amazes me how you know things before I ever arrive."

"Mother's never miss anything, I heard the Sheriff himself was at the school."

"Okay, let me start so you have all the facts," Maggie said with a chuckle. "Brandon Mitchell and Greg Swift failed to come in from recess. First we checked the building to be sure they were not hiding someplace inside. Then we called the Sheriff and let him know the situation. We put the building in lock-down to keep the other children safe and headed to the playground. We broke into teams of two and started walking. The Sheriff arrived just as we discovered someone had cut a section out of the fence. We went through the fence and spread out again. I heard whimpering so we stopped. The Sheriff spotted the two boys up a tree. Greg climbed down and the Sheriff went up to bring Brandon down. Greg was unhurt and Brandon has a broken arm. Both boys were sent home with their parents."

"Well, it certainly sounds like an interesting day."

"It was, but I'd rather not have any more like it," Maggie said honestly.

"What did Mr. Whitehead have to say?"

"You know, it puzzles me. This morning he called raving because he thought I hired someone to look into the school break-in. This afternoon when I called to report the incident, he was very complimentary."

"Well, maybe the man has some brains after all."

"Mom, he's not an idiot. He's got three buildings to deal with."

"Just like you to defend the man who threatened to take away your job," Estelle said disgustedly.

"I'm not defending him; just trying to understand him."

"If you say so, I have plans for the evening; do you want me to fix you some dinner before I go?"

"Heavens, no! I can still cook. Besides I want to give Marty a call."

"If you're sure, I'm going to go and get ready."

"Go, have fun."

Maggie walked to the phone and Estelle went to get ready for the evening.

"Hey, Marty," Maggie said when her brother answered the phone, "do you have any free time in the next week?" She paused for his answer, "That's great! I want to look at houses and I need to empty the house in Davenport." The pause was longer then she said, "Great, I'll be ready. See you then, my love to the kids and Ellen. Bye." She hung up the phone and headed for her bedroom and a quick change.

By the time she had showered and changed, Estelle was gone. Maggie made her way to the kitchen to see what she could scare up for dinner. She heard a knock at the back door and called out, "Come on in."

She looked surprised to see Sheriff Terry Norton come through the back door. Once she recovered she asked, "What can I do for you, Sheriff?"

"You can start by calling me, Terry," he said. "I owe you an apology and I'd like to take you out to dinner. Would it be okay?"

Maggie hesitated only a moment then said, "If I don't have to go and change."

"You look great the way you are," Terry said, blushing.

"Okay, let me write a note to Mom and we can be off."

Maggie wrote a quick note to her mother, grabbed a sweater and the two of them were out the back door. Terry held the door to his truck for her as she climbed in. She had to wonder at why the Sheriff thought he owed her an apology and decided it had to do with his initial interrogation of her. Whatever the reason, a night out would be good for her and would give her some time to ponder this sudden change in his attitude.

They drove to a quiet little restaurant on the outskirts of town appropriately named The Hideaway. As they got out of the truck, the Sheriff said, "I didn't want too many of the locals talking."

"I'm sure word will be out soon enough, let's just enjoy the evening."

Once inside they were seated in a small alcove where they could see without being seen. Maggie was shocked to see her mother and Dr. Gordon come in holding hands. She stifled a gasp as her mother looked her way.

In an instant, Estelle was steaming her way across the restaurant. "Maggie, what are you doing here?" she hissed.

"The same as you and Dr. Gordon, I believe, having dinner. You do know Sheriff Norton don't you?"

Estelle turned to the Sheriff and nodded. "This is not amusing, Margaret. We'll talk about this later." She turned and flounced back to where the good Doctor was waiting with an amused expression on his face.

"I suppose she'll want to give you a grilling when you get home," Terry mused.

"I'll say, imagine trying to keep a date with Dr. Gordon a secret. Did she think I would object?"

"Maybe she wasn't ready to go public," suggested Terry.

"Whatever her reason, we came to have dinner."

The waitress showed up then, Maggie ordered a Tom Collins and the Sheriff had Bud on tap. They ordered the bar-bequed ribs and salads. The waitress left and Terry found himself watching Maggie wondering how he could have been so wrong about someone.

"So, what makes you think you owe me an apology?" Maggie asked.

"You're not even going to let me get a drink first?" he chuckled. "Well, it's like this; I'm not from Timberview so I don't have all it's history. When you called to report a break-in at the school in the middle of the afternoon, I really thought you were nuts. The guys convinced me you had been frightened, but I still thought maybe you weren't all there."

The waitress brought their drinks. Maggie took a sip and nodded for him to continue. He took a gulp of his beer and went on, "Then when someone really did break-in to the school I wondered if you were in on it. Someone mentioned you had dated Howard in high school. I thought maybe it was a lover's spat. I knew you'd come here under some cloud, but I had no idea your family had been murdered."

Maggie continued to sip her drink and watch the Sheriff as he spoke. He seemed sincere, but she just wasn't sure.

Their salads arrived and they didn't talk for a few minutes as they ate. As soon as Terry was finished he started in again.

"When you walked into my office looking cool and collected, I thought you were a part of some conspiracy. I wasn't very kind to you. Then you left so abruptly, I knew I'd upset you and I wanted to know everything about you. I ran a background check and in the process ran into Erika Estwick. You couldn't have chosen a better person to look into things for you."

"Thank you it was my mother's doing."

The main course arrived and they dove into the ribs. Both agreed they were the best either one had ever had.

"Do you come here often?" Maggie surprised herself by asking.

"Nope this is the first time. I asked around about an out of the way place to take someone. It will have the Sheriff's Department talking for days." He smiled.

Maggie smiled back thinking it had been a long time since she shared a meal with any man but Ben.

"So, to finish my apology, I am sorry I thought you were here to stir up trouble in my town."

"Apology accepted," Maggie said warmly. "So, did you have anything to do with Mr. Whitehead's about face in attitude?"

"I called him while you were with the boys and calling their parents. I think I was partly to blame for him coming down on you so hard to begin with. I really was trying to make amends," he said somewhat sheepishly.

"It's not a problem. In fact, it was nice not to be yelled at when reporting an incident."

"Good, I did something right then." Terry raised his glass in a toast and Maggie joined him. They declined dessert and left quietly. Her mother and Dr. Gordon were still enjoying their meal.

"Is there anyplace you want to go before I take you home?" he asked hopefully.

"Not tonight, but I do thank you for a lovely evening."

"Let me know if there is anything you need help with."

"Come to think of it, my brother and I are going to Davenport on Saturday to clean out my house. I've rented a U-haul. We're going to store most of it in Marty's garage until I can find a place. Feel like some heavy lifting?"

"You tell me when to be there."

"We should be at the house around 10 am. Do you need directions or do you want to follow us?"

"I know where the house is, I'll meet you there."

Having made the decision to help, Terry held the door and helped Maggie into his truck then took her home. He walked her to the door and said his good-bye.

Once inside, Maggie had a lot to think about. First how long had her mother been seeing Dr. Gordon? Did Marty know? Why did she think she had to hide it? Why did Terry Norton know where her house in Davenport was? Finally, how soon could she find a house of her own?

She made her way to her bedroom, put on pajamas, and then went to the kitchen to put water on to boil. Once she had her cup of tea, she took a book and curled up in her bed. She knew her mother would come in when she returned home.

Maggie heard the door slam and knew Estelle was home. She looked at the clock to find it only a little past ten. She hadn't expected her mother this soon.

Estelle came into the room in a huff. "Just who do you think you are following me when I go out?" she demanded.

"Slow down, Mom, I wasn't following you. I had planned to stay in until Sheriff Norton showed up."

"And about Sheriff Norton, what were you doing on a date with him? Your husband has hardly been buried three months!" Estelle's voice grew increasingly louder with each word.

"I'm not going to talk to you when you are like this. Go to bed." Maggie set her book on the night stand and turned out the light.

"Margaret Ellen, turn the light on this instant!"

Calmly Maggie replied, "As soon as you rein in your temper and speak civilly, otherwise, I'm going to bed. I do have to be at work in the morning."

"Hrrummph," Estelle grumbled as she left the room.

Maggie smothered her laughter in her pillow then rolled over and went to bed. She knew from long experience she had not heard the end of this, but she also knew she no longer wanted to get into shouting matches with her mother over anything as trivial as being at the same place for dinner.

Maggie was out running before Estelle left her bedroom. She had taken to running earlier since school had actually started. She was surprised to find she was joined by Sheriff Norton.

"To what do I owe this?" she asked as she ran.

"Just protecting and serving one of the community members," he replied as he matched her pace.

"Yeah, right, when was the last time you were up this early jogging?"

"Actually I usually jog after work, thought I'd try something new."

"Going to give the town gossips something else to hold over my head are you?"

"Hadn't planned to, but it might be interesting to see what they make of this. Besides, I am avoiding all the single women who jog in the evening."

Maggie stopped in her tracks and laughed until she cried. "So, the old biddies are trying to set you up with their daughters. How long has this been going on?"

"Just the two months since I took this job."

They picked up the pace again and as Maggie made her way toward home Terry turned toward the Sheriff's Department.

Her mother had coffee going and the tea kettle on when she entered the back door.

"Honestly, Maggie, are you bent on causing a scandal?"

"No, Mom," Maggie replied without stopping as she headed toward her bedroom and a shower. When she was dressed, she went back to the kitchen for breakfast.

"First you have dinner with the Sheriff and then you go out jogging with him. What are you thinking?" Estelle picked up as if Maggie had never left the room.

Maggie rolled her eyes, and then said, "Mom, I am a grown woman. The Sheriff came to apologize last night and treated me to dinner. I did not expect to see him while I was jogging, but it was nice to have the company. It's all there is to it. While we are on the subject, when were you going to tell me you and Doc Gordon are an item?"

"It is none of your business," Estelle said indignantly.

"Does Marty know?"

"He does not, as it is none of his business either."

"Mom, you are a woman. Dad has been gone for ten years. If you want to have a life and share it with someone, Marty and I will not stand in your way."

"I am not having this discussion with you, Margaret."

"You can not have this conversation all you want. I will be late coming home as I am going house hunting."

Maggie grabbed a piece of toast from the counter and left. Speechless, Estelle just stood there gaping.

Maggie fumed all the way to work. She did not see why her mother was making such a big deal out of things. First thing she would do is ask Hope for the best realtor in town so she could start looking tonight. She wanted to be moved in to a place of her own as soon as possible.

She smiled as she entered the office, but Hope could tell Maggie was out of sorts. She decided to let it pass; Maggie would tell her if it was school related.

Maggie smiled when she saw Hope had put the tea on for her. She poured herself a cup and took a deep breath. Then she walked back into the outer office.

"Hope, do you know a good realtor?" she asked.

"Sure, when do you want to start looking?"

Maggie looked at her quizzically. "Tonight would be great! How soon can you put me in touch with this person?"

Hope smiled and said, "I just did."

"What do you mean?"

"I have done real estate sales part-time since before I got married. Let me call and make arrangements for the kids and we can leave as soon as you are ready."

Maggie laughed. "Hope, I have taken you for granted. You are so much more than a secretary." She headed back to her office. The day wasn't going to be so bad after all.

Maggie sat at her desk and made a list of things she'd like to have in a house. It sure would be different from the house in Davenport. On her list she included.

- At least two bedrooms
- A dishwasher
- A garage
- Hardwood floors would be nice
- Air conditioning
- A laundry room
- A bath and a half

This should about do it she thought. She could make one bedroom an at home office and still put a bed in it in case she had company. Then she laughed and wondered who this 'company' might be who would spend the night, maybe her nieces or nephews.

Maggie looked at the clock in time to see she needed to make the rounds and greet each teacher before going out to greet the busses. She only stopped in each room long enough to say "Hi." She remembered how busy the mornings were.

The students stopped on the way in to tell her about their adventures and give her hugs. She hugged them back and sent them on their way. This is the way every morning should start she thought. She waved to the bus drivers as she followed the last child into the building. She looked toward Hope to see if she had anything urgent. Seeing Hope was talking to a child, she began once again to walk through the building. She wanted the children to get used to seeing her in the hallways.

As the final bell rang, Maggie headed back to the office. Hope told her there was nothing pressing so she looked at the enrollment and the attendance to make sure all the students who were supposed to be there were in attendance. She was surprised to see neither of the Bright boys had been in attendance yesterday. She walked out to talk to Hope about it.

"Hope, do you know anything about the Bright family?" Maggie asked.

"You mean Caylee and her two boys?"

"Yes."

"Well, Caylee lives in a trailer out off Route 22. The boys are well behaved and get good grades. Why do you ask?"

"She approached me at the meeting Thursday night and told me both her boys would be in school yesterday. They weren't."

Hope nodded, "I guess you haven't heard. Caylee's newest boyfriend beat her up pretty bad. She's in the hospital and the boys are staying with relatives until she can come home."

"My goodness, what hospital is she in? I'll stop by to see her and find out if there is anyway we can transport the boys to school and back to the relatives until she is on her feet again."

"She'd be happy for them, but I'm not sure she wants you to see her all beat up."

"Let me worry about it."

Maggie went to her office and called the local hospital. Yes, they had a Caylee Bright and yes, she could have visitors from 6pm to 8:30pm. Maggie thanked them and hung up the phone.

She dialed her mother's and got the answering machine. So, she left a message she would be late coming in tonight not to save her any dinner.

She'd barely set the phone down when it rang again. "Mrs. Parsons," she said when she answered the phone.

"Okay, so what did you and Mom fight about this time?"

"Nice to hear from you too, Marty?" Maggie shot back at him.

"What is the problem?" asked her exasperated brother.

"I went out to dinner last night and saw Mom with Doc Gordon. I guess they are an item."

"Of course they are. She's been seeing him for a couple of years."

"Well, she thinks she's keeping it a secret from you. I also told her I'm going to look for my own place."

"Good for you. I wondered how long the two of you would last together."

Maggie hesitated then said, "It's not because we aren't getting along. Mom and I are getting along better than I thought we would. I need to move on, Marty and build a new life."

"I'm glad to hear you say so, Sis. I was getting worried you'd hang onto the past forever."

"I've put the house up for sale and Sheriff Norton has offered to come by on Saturday and help us load up a U-haul."

"Great, we can get all the big stuff moved. Where are you going to put it?"

"I'm going out tonight to see if I can find something I might be able to move into by Saturday."

"Good luck. I'll see you then."

"Thanks, Marty, hope you have a good afternoon." Maggie hung up the phone smiling. She wondered how many people knew about her mother and Doc Gordon.

The day went much more smoothly than the first. Maggie and her staff walked the children to their busses and stood there as they drove away.

"I hope every day is like this one," Ginny said wistfully.

"From your lips to God's ears," replied Mrs. Feldstein.

"Well, troops, do what you have to, but I'm all for calling it a day," Maggie said as they made their way inside.

Hope was waiting for her. She held an envelope in her hands.

"What's that?"

"I'm not sure. I went to use the restroom as you walked the kids out and it was on my desk when I came back."

"Did you open it?"

"No, it said confidential on it."

"I think I'll take it to my office."

"I'm coming with you."

They walked to Maggie's office where they both found seats. Maggie slit the envelope open with a letter opener. Out fell one sheet of paper. On it were words to stop Maggie's heart.

> *Yesterday was easy. Next time you won't be so lucky.*

"Oh, my God!" said Hope.

Maggie was dialing 911 when she looked up and saw Sheriff Norton coming through the front doors. She put the phone down and ran toward him, shouting at Hope, "Don't touch it!"

The Sheriff looked toward the office and knew by the look on Maggie's face something was terribly wrong. He entered the office just as she did.

"What's wrong, Maggie?"

"Letter, we got a letter." She turned and fled back toward her office.

Hope was still standing where Maggie had left her, one hand covering her mouth the other over her heart.

Sheriff Norton rounded the desk to look at the piece of paper lying there. "Who has touched this?"

Maggie found her voice and said, "No one has touched the piece of paper, but Hope and I both held the envelope."

"Your prints are on file as part of the job and so are Hope's. Anyone else's will be our suspect." He picked up the phone and called his office. I need a crime unit at the elementary school ASAP. No lights or sirens just get here."

Maggie sank into the chair next to where Hope was standing. "This is a bad joke. Does someone mean to harm the students?"

"Has the fence been mended?"

"It was this morning before the first kids went outside."

"Good, now we have to figure out how they got in and out of here without being seen."

"Is Austin Howard still in jail?"

"No, he's out on bail."

"I cannot believe he'd go after children," Maggie said.

"Sheriff, do Maggie and I have to stay?" Hope asked.

"No, but I want the rest of the staff to leave too. Do you want to tell them Maggie or do you want me to?"

"I'll make an announcement," Maggie said and walked to the front office and the PA system. She punched a few numbers and then said, "Staff, I need you all to gather your things and lock your rooms. I'll meet you in the parking lot in five minutes."

"Thanks, Maggie. I'll come by later and let you know what we find out."

"It might be better if you call me on my cell phone. I have some errands I'm running tonight and I don't know when I'll get home." She handed him a scrap of paper with her cell phone number on it. Then she and Hope shut everything up and headed toward the parking lot.

Several teachers had put things in their cars and were milling around.

"Let's gather around the flag pole," Maggie suggested.

Quietly they walked to the flag pole and Maggie told them what had happened. "I don't believe we are in any danger at the moment. I do believe someone has access to our building. I want you to be very vigilant about where your students are at all times. I'm going to try to make it out for part of each recess. If any of you are willing to spend time with your class during recess, it would be appreciated. I know it is your prep time, but right now the children's safety is the big concern. If it is a union issue I will see what I can do to get you compensated."

Several told Maggie they would volunteer their time to keep the kids safe. Those reluctant proposed they rotate the teachers who were out and who were in. This way they would be patrolling inside and out. Many thought it was a good idea and they agreed to draw up a rotation schedule and bring it to Maggie in the morning.

It was Mrs. Feldstein who said, "Maggie, you cannot be every place at once. Let us do the rotating. You handle your job."

"Thank you," Maggie said once again overwhelmed by the thoughtfulness of her staff. "I am off to visit Caylee Bright and see if we can arrange to get her two boys back in school while she is recovering. I will let you know what develops. Have a good evening. See you all in the morning."

They headed toward their cars. The crime unit had arrived while Maggie was talking to them. Many were speculating on who could want to hurt the children as they walked away.

"Maggie, let me drive," Hope said. I have the keys I need and we can just go from place to place."

"Sounds good to me I made a list of the things I'd like to have."

"Then let's be off." They walked to Hope's car and set out on the search for the perfect house.

The first stop had been at the florists, where Maggie picked out a modest bouquet of flowers and then they headed toward the hospital. Caylee Bright was on the second floor. She looked so small in the bed Maggie wanted to cry. Her face was bruised and swollen.

"Aw you shouldn't have done that," Caylee said through her wired jaw.

"I came to see how you were and to see if there is any way we can get the boys in school."

"They're staying with my ma in Kirkridge. It's too far for her to get them here and then get to work."

"What if I find someone to transport them back and forth to school?"

"It would be great! I hate for them to be missin'."

"I'll work on it and call your mother when we have a plan. In the meantime you just rest and get well.

Caylee tried to smile. The effort cost her, but she managed to say, "Thank you, Miz Parsons."

"You're welcome, Caylee. We'll leave you alone now. Is there anything you need?"

"No, I got all I need."

The two women left the room. Hope thinking Maggie was taking on something not her problem and Maggie believing she had just lifted a burden from another woman.

On the ground floor Maggie said, "I'm all yours Madame Real Estate Woman, let's find me a house."

They were off on a mission from then on. Maggie was getting tired of looking at houses when they drove to the fourth one on the list.

The fourth house was the keeper. It was nestled off the road down a winding lane. It had a stream in the back yard which had been made to form a natural pool. It was a red brick ranch with white trim. There was an attached garage with a walkway through to the house. Maggie could easily picture it as a mud room and the previous owners had put a half bath and shower in there. You entered into the laundry/furnace room, then into the kitchen. It was a nice size kitchen. From there you took a hall to the three bedrooms and bath or just walked into the living room.

"I don't care how much it is," Maggie said joyously, "this is the house I want."

"Then we'll run by my house so I can pick up the paperwork and get everything done over dinner."

"How soon do you think I could move in?"

"It's ready to go now unless you want to do some cleaning and painting."

"I can live with the paint for a while, I love the hardwood floors. I can do a quick cleaning it's no problem. Can I start moving things in on Saturday?"

"I'll make the call at dinner and we'll see."

The two women locked the door and left for Hope's home office. It was then Maggie's cell phone chirped.

"Hello."

"Maggie, this is Sheriff Norton."

"What did you find?"

"Nothing just like we expected. I want to put a plain clothes person in your building for a few days."

"How are they going to blend in?"

"I thought about it, and then I called Mr. Whitehead. We are going to put one of my people in as a principal trainee."

"Okay, sounds good, what time will he be arriving?"

"We don't want to scare the person off so; I'm sending Officer Amy Welsh in tomorrow. What time do you want her to arrive?"

"Have her there at 7:45 for the staff meeting."

"She'll be there."

"Thank you."

"No problem."

Maggie snapped her phone shut, "Do we have an office anywhere in the building the I can put an assistant?"

"There is an old office in the fourth and fifth grade wing."

"Good, it's where we are going to put my new trainee tomorrow."

"Trainee?"

"Yes, it seems the note today has everyone a bit suspicious and the Sheriff is putting an undercover policewoman in our building as a principal trainee."

"It will make people happy and also give us extra eyes and ears."

"Yes and she is being introduced to the staff as a trainee, we are not telling anyone else she is undercover."

"Okay by me. Can we get her a phone line and I'll send some of the easier calls her way."

"We'll work on it. We have the two-way for now."

Hope sighed. "Let's forget school for tonight, get those papers and have some celebration dinner."

"Yes, let's."

The two went on to Hope's, picked up the papers and Hope found the owner's phone number, then they went to The Hideaway for dinner.

Hope called the owner while they waited for their drinks to come. She was smiling when she hung up the phone.

"Well," said Maggie anxiously.

"The owner will agree to your price and says you can move in tomorrow if it suits you."

Maggie lifted her iced tea in a toast. Hope joined her by lifting her Coke. Then the two relaxed and enjoyed their dinner.

"How did you know about this place?" Hope asked.

"Well, Sheriff Norton came by last night to offer an apology for the first time we met and brought me here."

"It's nice, going to get my husband to bring me here on our next night out."

"You schedule nights out?"

"You bet I do. With three kids, you have to have some time alone. We hire a sitter about once every two weeks and spend some time just enjoying each other."

"What a neat idea."

"You and your husband never did?"

Maggie sighed, "Ben and I were so tuned to each others needs we never felt like we needed to be away. Sometimes getting away for us was putting the twins to bed and sitting on the back porch watching the stars."

"Oh, how romantic."

"I guess it was. I never thought of it."

Their meals came and they stopped talking long enough to eat.

It had been a pleasant evening. Hope drove back to the school so Maggie could pick up her car. They were dumbfounded at the sight in front of them. On the side of Maggie's car was spray painted: Go Home Traitor.

Hope was the first to call 9-1-1. She gave the location and the problem. They could hear the sirens almost immediately.

Maggie sat there stunned. Who was she a traitor to and this was her home. What was going on? Who was behind this? Why were they doing this?

The first to arrive was Sheriff Norton. Maggie was surprised to see Erika Estwick get out of the passenger side of his car. The three of them walked to Maggie's car. Erika took some pictures with her ever present digital camera.

"Maggie, was this here at the end of the day?"

"No, the car was fine when we left."

"Do you often leave your car here after hours?"

"No, this is the first time. Hope and I were going house hunting."

"Did you touch the car when you got back?"

"No, we called you."

"Good, I'm going to have your car impounded so we can see if there are any fingerprints. Do you have a way home?"

"Yes, Hope can drop me off."

"Can I get your car keys? We'll have the paint cleaned off and I'll return it to you as soon as we are done with it."

Maggie reached for her key ring and took the ignition key off. She handed it to Sheriff Norton.

Erika walked over to where Maggie and the Sheriff were standing. "The paint is tempera. It won't withstand a good rain. Maggie, can I come by the house when things are wrapped up here? I have a couple of questions for you."

"Sure, Hope is going to drive me home. I'll be waiting for you."

"Okay I'll see you in a few minutes." Erika walked toward the patrolman who was talking to the tow truck driver.

Hope took Maggie's arm. "Let's get you home," she said as she guided Maggie back to her car.

"Hope, why does someone think I'm a traitor? Who is doing this?"

"You know, I haven't got a clue, but I think the Sheriff will be on this until he knows."

The two women drove the short distance to Maggie's mothers. "Do you want to come inside?"

"Not tonight, I think your mom is going to have enough on her hands."

Maggie stood there watching as Hope drove away. Had it just been an hour ago they were celebrating her purchase of a new house? She slowly turned to go inside.

"M aggie," Estelle called when she heard her daughter enter the back door, "I didn't hear you drive up." As she spoke she walked to the kitchen. "My God, Maggie what has happened now?

Maggie sat at the counter. She looked at her mother and said, "I don't know where to start, but Erika Estwick will be here shortly."

"Did she learn something to upset you?"

"I don't know. She said she had a couple of questions."

"So where is your car?"

"The police impounded it."

Estelle was beside herself trying to make sense of what Maggie was saying. "You'd better start at the beginning."

"Hope and I went out after work looking at houses. We found one and I've put a down payment on it." Maggie looked up when her mother gasped, and then she continued, "We had dinner and when we got back to the school to pick up my car, the side of it was painted with the word 'TRAITOR' in big letters. Hope called the police. Sheriff Norton arrived with Erika and it's all I know." Maggie shook her head as if unable to comprehend what had happened.

Estelle said nothing and put the kettle on to make tea. She had an uneasy feeling something else bad was going to happen. She took three cups down from the cupboard. She also reached for the whiskey. Erika seemed to know when Maggie needed it and so did Estelle. Although she would wait until Erika had asked her questions before serving any.

Maggie was sitting in her father's chair when Erika arrived twenty minutes later. Estelle ushered her in.

"Maggie, the sheriff told me to tell you the car would be brought back around noon tomorrow. They'll bring it to the school," she began.

Maggie just nodded, she was feeling numb. Estelle tried to make everyone at ease by offering to get some tea.

"None for me, thanks, Mrs. Mills," Erika said. "I just need to ask Maggie a couple of questions?"

"Fire away," Maggie said with a half-hearted laugh.

"What do you know about Laura Gilbert's first year of college?"

"Not much. We went to different colleges. We wrote and were together at homecoming. She complained about professors and told me about the cute guys in the library, but I was telling her pretty much the same kind of stuff."

"Did you know she had been seeing Austin Howard?"

"No, but it wouldn't have been a big deal. We all hung out together in high school."

"How did you lose touch with her?"

"Well, it seems my mother and Ashton's learned Laura was pregnant and told her we wanted nothing to do with her. I didn't know anything about it until a week or two ago."

Erika turned to Estelle, "Mrs. Mills, what made the two of you tell Laura the girls didn't want to hear from her?"

Estelle blushed then said, "We didn't want our girls distracted from their studies. Both of us sent money to help Laura out."

"In other words, you felt she had shamed herself?"

"Yes."

"Thank you both for your time. I'll get back to you in a week or so and let you know if I have turned up anything worth pursuing." She stood to leave.

Estelle walked her to the door. Erika turned and said, "I think some of Grandma's recipe is in order for Maggie tonight."

"Yes, I have it ready."

Erika nodded then left.

The morning started off uneventful. Maggie was grateful to her staff for giving her a rotation schedule for lunch and recess. It was an hour until lunch, when a student came into the office asking Mrs. Parson's to come to her room it was an emergency. Maggie didn't ask questions she just went.

She found Mrs. Feldstein's first grade classroom sitting silently in their chairs. One chair was markedly empty.

"What is the problem, Mrs. Feldstein?" Maggie asked quietly.

"We just returned from using the restroom and washing up for lunch and Jacob Mitchell didn't return. We have searched the bathroom and everywhere else we can think of, but he's gone," she replied wringing her hands. "I'm so sorry, this has happened."

"Not to worry," Maggie assured her. "You just keep to your schedule and we will search the whole building with as little disruption as possible."

A small little boy raised his hand then said, "He went in the secret door."

Maggie was instantly alert, "Can you show me the secret door?"

He nodded and walked to Maggie. The two of them left the room.

She quietly asked, "Has Jacob gone to the secret room before?"

"Just once, I think. I told him not to go."

"I'm sure you did. Can you tell me your name?"

"I'm Ryan Sacks," he answered proudly.

"This is a very brave thing you are doing, Ryan."

Maggie took the walkie-talkie from her belt and asked Hope to send the custodian to meet her. They appeared to be headed for the lower level restrooms.

The custodian arrived just as Maggie and Ryan did. They checked to make sure no one was in the boys' restroom and then the three of them entered. Ryan quickly took them to a door concealed in the wall of the restroom.

"Well, I'll be," Mr. Honeywell said. "I thought this had been taken out years ago."

"Where does it lead?" Maggie asked.

"To the old boiler room and some underground tunnels," he replied. "We're going to need some flashlights. You wait right here."

Maggie turned to Ryan, "I need you to do a very special job. I need you to keep everyone out of this bathroom. Can you stand guard for me?"

Ryan beamed from ear to ear and nodded his assent. Then he went to stand just outside the bathroom door to keep others out.

Mr. Honeywell arrived with two large flashlights and an old yellowed building plan. He handed Maggie a flashlight and rolled the building plan out.

"I told Hope to call the Sheriff and have him come quietly over. I want him here just in case our boy is hurt or stuck someplace."

"Good thinking, I need to let our little guard know the Sheriff can enter," Maggie said walking to the door. She relayed the message to Ryan and returned.

"You stick close to me, Mrs. Parsons. I don't want to have to be looking for two people."

"I will, let's go."

They opened the old door and entered. It was musty smelling and there was a lot of dust.

"Looky here," Mr. Honeywell pointed to footprints in the dust.

They would be able to follow Jacob's footprints and hopefully find him unharmed. They walked slowly looking into every dark crevice they came to. There was no sign of Jacob. Maggie could feel the hairs on the back of her neck starting to stand up. Something was very wrong, she could feel it. She gave a slight scream when someone touched her on the back.

"I'm sorry I frightened you," the Sheriff said.

Maggie immediately felt a sense of relief. Help had arrived. She still had an uneasy feeling something was wrong.

It's when Mr. Honeywell let out a long whistle. There were several sets of footprints and none of them were child size. Where had Jacob gotten to and who else had been here?

They continued on and discovered the tunnel led to an old shed at the back of the school property and inside a fence. No one was surprised to see the fence had been cut.

Sheriff Norton radioed the police station and asked to have someone come out from the crime lab. They needed fingerprints.

Mr. Honeywell found some footprints and tire tracks. The Sheriff left him in charge and walked back to the school with Maggie.

"I'm going to have to call Matt Mitchell and tell him his son is missing," Maggie said regretfully.

"I'm going to put out an amber alert. Do you have a school photo we can use?"

"Sure, I'll have Hope get it," she spoke into her walkie-talkie, "Hope, I need you to get a school photo of Jacob Mitchell ready and get Mr. Mitchell on the phone for me. Oh, yes, and can you find a treat for Ryan Sacks and send him back to class? Thanks."

Maggie and the Sheriff walked in silence the rest of the way. Maggie wondering who was behind this and why Matt's boys were involved. The phone conversation she was going to have with Matt would not be pleasant.

Maggie took off her walkie-talkie as she entered the office. She handed it to Hope and told her as soon as she had spoken to Matt Mitchell, she needed to talk to Mr. Whitehead. It was another call she was dreading.

The Sheriff followed Maggie to her office. He got them both coffees as she picked up her phone and pushed the blinking light.

"Matt, this is Maggie Parsons at the school," her voice sounded calm in spite of the tension in her stomach. "I need you and your wife to come to the school as quickly as you can."

She paused listening to Matt then said, "I need to talk to you both in person. It is important you come now."

Again she paused, "I'll be waiting."

Another light blinked on the phone as she finished the call and hung up.

"Put Mr. Whitehead on the speaker phone," the Sheriff said.

Maggie picked up the phone, "Mr. Whitehead, Sheriff Norton is here and asked me to put you on the speaker." She hit the speaker button as she spoke.

"What is going on there now?" Mr. Whitehead roared.

"Calm yourself," the Sheriff said, "Mrs. Parsons and I have discovered how people keep getting into this building."

"Well, finally some good news. How soon can we get it closed off?"

"Just as soon as the crime scene technicians have cleared it."

"Crime scene technicians! Some one had better tell me what is going on right now!" he sputtered.

Maggie spoke first, "Jacob Mitchell has gone missing. We followed his trail in the underground tunnel. I have a call into Mr. and Mrs. Mitchell. They are on their way here."

"Mrs. Parsons, this is unacceptable. First, there is a break in, then two boys go missing and one ends up with a broken arm. I've heard about your car being spray painted, and now this!" Maggie could picture Mr. Whitehead's face turning all shades of purple as he spewed and sputtered about her incompetence.

The Sheriff spoke gruffly into the phone, "I don't believe any of this has to do with Mrs. Parsons' competency. This has to do with neglect on the part of the school district. The door should have been sealed off years ago and it is a wonder we haven't lost more children through it. The fence had been cut and boys will be boys. There was no way anyone could have predicted they would climb a tree and get stuck."

"Well," Mr. Whitehead said, "I guess I'll be called on to make some kind of statement."

"Not yet, Mr. Whitehead," the Sheriff responded. "I want to put out an amber alert and we are going to put the school into lockdown until time to go home. There will be no children on the playground and only those adults who are on the children's emergency cards will be allowed to sign them out. Mrs. Parsons already has her staff doing extra security checks. This child went missing during a classroom bathroom break. His teacher was there."

"I should fire that teacher."

"No, you should get your maintenance man out here pronto and get this problem fixed," replied the Sheriff sternly.

Mr. Whitehead disconnected and the office was silent. After a few minutes Maggie spoke, "What do you need me to do?"

Sheriff Norton turned to Maggie and said, "This is going to be very tough on you. We need to get the media here now. I will make a statement, the Mitchells will make a statement, we will get Jacob's photo out there and get the Amber Alert going. You are going to be bombarded with calls from anxious parents. Don't be surprised if many come for their kids. I will do everything I can to let them know we have the safety of the children as our priority."

Maggie felt her stomach clutch. "I suppose I had better make a statement, too."

"It would be a good idea. I have Amy Walsh on the way over. You might introduce her as your new second in command and then I'll put her in your office answering phone calls."

"Hope gets all the calls first. Should I just have her send them to Amy?"

"Yes, then you will be visible in the school. Go to lunch with the kids."

"I suspect the Mitchells will want to take Brandon home."

"It won't be a problem, but it might be better if he kept to his normal schedule. Let's wait and talk to them."

Maggie jumped when the phone buzzed. She picked it up. "This is Maggie Parsons. Yes, Hope, send them both in."

She hung up the phone, looked at the Sheriff, and said, "Matt Mitchell and his wife are here."

The Mitchells walked into Maggie's office. She offered them a seat and some coffee.

"I'm surprised to see the Sheriff here, did Brandon run off again?" Matt said as he took the cup of coffee from Maggie.

"No, this has nothing to do with Brandon. I don't quite know how to say this, but Jacob is missing."

Mrs. Mitchell gasp and her hand shook.

"I don't understand," Matt said.

Sheriff Norton spoke up, "What we have determined is Jacob found a door to the old boiler room in the boys' bathroom. He's gone in before. Today he went in and someone has taken him."

"What do you mean taken my son!" Mrs. Mitchell screamed and then began to cry.

"How did this happen? He's supposed to be safe here," Matt accused.

"We don't know yet," the Sheriff said. "What we have to do right now is concentrate on finding him and getting him back. I have the local news station coming in a few minutes and I'm going to make a statement. I'd like a statement from you or your wife and I want you to show Jacob's school photo. We are going to issue an Amber Alert. Then Mrs. Parsons will make a statement."

Matt had the stunned look of a deer in the headlights. He hardly knew how to respond. "Who would take Jacob? Why would they take Jacob? He knows not to go with strangers." He turned on Maggie and said, "How did you let this happen? We supported you when you said to give you a chance the kids would be safe. So far, Brandon has a broken arm and now Jacob is missing. What do you have planned for Melanie?"

Maggie could feel his tension. He had to lash out at someone. She quietly said, "I'm sorry, Matt, I didn't mean for any of this to happen. I'm doing what I can to fix it."

Matt looked to Sheriff Norton, "What do you want?"

"Just as I said, I need you to make a plea to who ever took Jacob."

"I can do it," Matt said as he put his arm around his sobbing wife. "Andrea, do you want to hold the picture of Jacob?"

She nodded and continued sobbing.

Amy Walsh was waiting in the outer office when the Sheriff entered from Maggie's office. She wore a dove gray suit and her blonde hair was pulled up in a bun. She was all business when she asked, "How can I be of assistance?"

"Let me introduce you to Hope," he turned to the school secretary and said, "Hope, this is Amy Walsh, she is Mrs. Parsons' new assistant. Please screen all calls to her."

Hope stood and shook Amy's hand, "Welcome aboard. We have an office set up for you in the other end of the building. I'll switch any incoming calls to you. Let me show you where it is."

"Thank you."

The two women left the Sheriff standing in the office and went to the fourth and fifth grade wing of the building.

"I'm glad you are here," Hope said.

"I can see this is going to be a real quick break in day for me."

"Yes, Maggie had planned a staff meeting for the morning to introduce you. Ah, here we are," Hope indicated a door on the left. "I'm sorry I'm the only secretary. This office hasn't been used in a long time. You have your choice of inner or outer office."

Amy looked around and said, "Not bad, I think the outer office might be better. It will allow me to see into the hallway. Do you have a doorstop?"

Hope opened the bottom drawer of the desk and produced a rubber doorstop. "How's this?"

"Perfect, let me get settled in and can you tell me where I might get some coffee or water?"

Hope opened the door to the inner office. There on a table top was a coffee pot and a jug of water. In a small refrigerator under the table there was cold water and an assortment of pop as well as some cream. Then she opened a cupboard above the table and showed Amy where to find any kind of sweetener imaginable and some coffee mugs. In a drawer were spoons.

"You sure were prepared," Amy said impressed they had gone out of their way to make her feel like she really belonged.

"I put my extension and Maggie's on a pad by the phone. You will find note pads, pens, pencils and about any other office supply you can think of in the desk. We also have a small file cabinet in there for you to use. Let me know if you are missing something," Hope said, "I need to get back to the main office."

"Thanks again, I'll just make myself at home."

Hope went back to the office feeling as though they'd made a good decision in letting Amy Walsh become a part of the staff, even if it would only be for a short while.

**35**

The main office was starting to fill up. Sheriff Norton, Maggie and the Mitchells were all in the office when Hope got back.

Outside there was a commotion in the parking lot. News reporters from surrounding towns had picked up on the missing child bulletin. They were fighting for the best space.

Sheriff Norton looked at the three and said, "Is everybody ready?"

All responded by nodding yes. He looked at Hope and said, "I need you to have Amy Walsh down here by the time Maggie is ready to speak. The Mitchells are going to be in front of the camera first, then I will address them, and finally Maggie will make a statement and introduce Amy as the person they will be speaking with if they call the school."

"I'm on it," Hope said as she reached for the phone.

The four stepped outside into the late summer sunlight. Several reporters came forward as one. Mrs. Mitchell began a new round of sobbing and Maggie took one of her arms while Matt held the other.

The Sheriff held up his hand for silence and Matt Mitchell spoke his voice breaking with each word, "Someone has come

155

to the school and lured my son, Jacob away. I don't know why. I just know we want him back. If you have any information, please call the Sheriff's Department."

He paused and reached for his wife. Andrea Mitchell stepped up and held Jacob's picture out for everyone to see. She surprised everyone by saying, "This is Jacob. I want my son." She again broke into tears as Maggie and Matt helped her back toward the building.

Amy Walsh quietly showed up and walked back out with Maggie.

"This incident has not put any of the other children at risk. They are practicing shelter in place which means going about their normal day. They will stay in at recess so they can all be accounted for. Everything at the school is under control. We have issued an Amber Alert for Jacob with a description of what he was wearing today. We are looking for any tips which will be helpful in bringing Jacob back home."

As the Sheriff stepped back Maggie and Amy stepped up. "I am saddened someone has made the children targets in some sick game. I will do everything in my power to insure this does not happen again. I have an intern-assistant, Ms. Amy Walsh who will be fielding all calls to the school. Maintenance staff is on its way to take care of the building problem and make it secure so the people who took Jacob cannot get in again."

One reporter shouted, "Is this more of the trouble which has come to the school with you, Mrs. Parsons?"

"No trouble has come with me to the school."

Another fired off, "Wasn't the school broken into? Hasn't your car been vandalized, didn't two boys go missing on the first day of school?"

"One question at a time please," Maggie said her head throbbing. "First, the school was broken into, had nothing to do with me. Yes, my car was vandalized and the police are investigating it. Yes, two boys went through an opening in the school fence. They were found within minutes and the fence has been repaired."

Amy stepped up before anyone else could shout a question. "Mrs. Parsons has done all in her power to insure student safety. It is time the community start doing the same. Open your eyes and start looking for Jacob Mitchell. No further questions at this time."

All three turned and walked into the school as the reporters continued to fire questions, and make comments.

"You did a great job, Maggie," the Sheriff said.

Maggie nodded. She was starting to feel numb. "Is there someone who can go home with the Mitchells?"

"We have someone waiting at their home."

She walked into her office where Hope had ushered the Mitchells after the interview. Both Brandon and Melanie were with their parents.

Amy spoke up, "Mr. Mitchell, where is your car parked?"

Matt Mitchell looked up and hesitated before answering, "In the lot at the other end of the building"

"Great, you and your family come with the Sheriff and I, we will get you to your car without the reporters bothering you."

Matt Mitchell looked grateful. He helped Andrea up and hustled the children along in front of them. They made the long walk to their car.

Maggie sat for a minute in her chair and put her head in her hands. Her head ached and she felt drained. She felt almost as bad as when Ben and the kids died. How was she going to get through this? The Mitchells had trusted her. All the parents trusted her to protect their children and now this had happened.

The phone buzzed and Maggie slowly picked up the receiver, "This is Maggie Parsons."

"This is the Timberview Times, Mrs. Parsons."

"I gave my statement to the press just a few minutes ago," Maggie interrupted, "I have nothing more to say."

"No, Mrs. Parsons, we have a little boy who just wandered in with a note pinned to his shirt. He says his name is Jacob Mitchell."

"Don't touch the note, Sheriff Norton and I will be there as quick as we can." Maggie hung up the phone grabbed her purse and headed out of her office.

"Hope, page the Sheriff to this office NOW!"

Hope quickly got on the PA system and requested the Sheriff report to the main office immediately. She looked at Maggie, who shook her head and paced in the small space.

The Sheriff came at a run. He almost collided with the door Maggie pushed open. "Whoa, where's the fire?"

"At the Timberview Press, they have Jacob Mitchell."

The Sheriff stopped and stared. "What do you mean they have Jacob Mitchell?"

"They just called and said he wandered in with a note pinned to his shirt and said he was Jacob Mitchell. Let's not stand here, let's go and get him." Maggie charged her way out the front door.

"I'll drive, we'll take the squad car," he said. When Maggie looked at him strangely he continued, "I can put on the lights and siren and get us there faster."

Maggie nodded, changed directions and got into the front seat of the patrol car.

True to his word, the Sheriff put on the lights and siren and they raced the few blocks to the newspaper office. Both of them got out as soon as the car stopped.

Entering the newspaper office like a whirlwind, Maggie demanded to know where Jacob was.

"I'm right here, Mrs. Parsons," he said in a quiet voice.

Maggie turned to the sound of his voice. Her first instinct was to take him in her arms and cuddle him. Knowing it would destroy the note pinned to his shirt she refrained from hugging and pulled herself together to ask him, "Are you all right?"

"Sure, Mrs. Parsons, the man took me for an ice cream cone and then we went to the park and he dropped me off and told me to come here."

Sheriff Norton quickly asked, "What man, Jacob?"

"The one who went to school with Mrs. Parsons and used to work at the school," Jacob turned to look at Maggie, "Mrs. Parsons I think he's mad at you. He said it was okay if I went, but I didn't think I should without telling someone."

"Jacob, why do you think he's mad at Mrs. Parsons?" the Sheriff asked.

"He said Mrs. Parsons stole his happiness. I didn't really understand it," he paused then asked, "Sheriff, how do you steal happiness?"

"I'm not sure, Jacob, but when I know I'll tell you. Do you mind if I read your note?"

"Nope, the man said you would want to." Jacob smiled then said, "He put on gloves, too, but his were old work gloves."

Jacob had noticed the gloves Sheriff Norton had put on to keep from tampering with the evidence. Jacob's revelation meant there would probably be no usable fingerprints, but he was being cautious just in case.

The Sheriff asked one of the secretaries for a plastic cover to put the letter in. Once in there, he and Maggie read the note.

*See how easy it was. You cannot even keep the children safe. You are not fit to be in charge.*

Maggie dropped into the nearest chair. She could not speak for a moment.

Sheriff Norton quietly said, "Let's get Jacob home, then we'll work on the letter." He turned to the nearest person and asked, "May I use your phone, please?"

The young lady turned her phone around for him to use.

Sheriff Norton called his office, "I need you to call all the TV stations and newspapers who were represented at the press conference this afternoon. Tell them to be at the Mitchell's in thirty minutes. Also cancel the amber alert. We have Jacob." He hung up the phone and turned to Maggie and Jacob.

"So, Jacob, how would you like to ride in a police car?"

Jacob nodded his head enthusiastically.

"Maggie, would you like to come with us?"

Maggie nodded and rose from the chair. She felt as though she was walking in someone else's body. Her movements were mechanical.

Once settled in the squad car, the Sheriff said to Jacob, "I think we're going to run with both the lights and siren."

"Cool," Jacob said.

The ride to the Mitchell's was quick. Matt came to stand on the front porch when he heard the siren: he was prepared for the worst. His facial expression turned to stunned surprise when he saw Jacob run from the car. He turned to call out to his wife.

Maggie and the Sheriff hung back to watch the family reunion. Maggie wondered aloud, "How did we go from tragedy to triumph?"

"I suspect no one planned to harm him from the beginning. Someone is out to discredit you." He put his hand in the small of her back and forced her to approach the Mitchells.

"We need to go inside and talk," he said quietly. "The press will be here in about twenty minutes and we want to be ready for them."

Mrs. Mitchell led the way to the living room. She sat on the sofa with Jacob on her lap and the other two children on either side of her.

"You're not going to like what Jacob told us," the Sheriff started. "He said he went with a man worked with the school and who went to school with Mrs. Parsons. I assume he would also have gone to school with you, Mr. Mitchell."

Matt looked at Maggie. "Aussie?"

"It's what I think," she replied.

"But why?"

"According to Jacob, I stole his happiness. If the note attached to Jacob's shirt is to be taken as true, someone is out to discredit me."

"Glen Swift's kids attend the school and so does Ashton's little girl. Why was I singled out?" Matt wanted to know.

"We don't know the answer. We don't even know for sure who wrote the note or what it really means," the Sheriff replied. "You might want to consider keeping the kids home for a day or two."

Mrs. Mitchell spoke up, "No. School has just started. I trust Maggie. She did everything right or we wouldn't have Jacob home. My kids are going to school. No one has the right to threaten my children and we are not going to be driven away."

"All I can do until we get this figured out is beef up the road patrols around the school."

"It should take care of things," Matt said hopefully.

There was a commotion out front as the press started to show up. The Sheriff nodded and said, "Press is here. We are going to keep the contents of the note quiet. We are just going to make a statement Jacob has been returned."

"I'd like to make a statement," Matt said. "I want this guy to know he is messing with the wrong people."

"Mr. Mitchell, we cannot have you making threats."

"I don't intend to. I just want to show my support for the school and Mrs. Parsons."

"Okay, fine," Sheriff Norton said with reluctance.

They all walked out to meet the press. Mrs. Mitchell held Jacob in her arms. The other two children stood beside her. The Sheriff made his statement then Matt Mitchell spoke.

"I do not know who is responsible for taking my son today. I do know the Sheriff will bring the person to justice. In the meantime, my family and I will try to get our lives back to normal. Which includes sending my children to school. I believe Mrs. Parsons did everything in her power to make the children safe and she will continue to do so."

Although the reporters tried to get more, the Mitchells entered their home and Sheriff Norton told them the conference was over. He thanked them for their prompt response and promised to let them know when there was a break in the case.

Maggie had stood mute and off to the side during the whole thing.

"Mrs. Parsons, do you want to make a statement?"

A chorus of yes followed and cameras and microphones were shoved toward Maggie.

"At this time, I am just glad we have a happy ending." Maggie turned heading toward the squad car.

Sheriff Norton joined her and they headed for her mother's.

"I have to go back to the school and get my car," Maggie protested.

"Not tonight you don't. You need to go home and rest."

"I need to tell my staff Jacob is safe. I need to brief them."

"It's why you have an assistant. She took care of it while we were taking Jacob home. Maggie, this is not your fault. I will find out who is behind this and we will put an end to it."

Maggie closed her eyes. She fought the tears burning the back of her eyelids. She needed to rest. She'd feel better in the morning. Somehow she couldn't make herself believe it.

When they arrived at her mother's Maggie quietly thanked the Sheriff for bringing her home and made her way in the back door.

Estelle had the tea kettle on. She turned to Maggie and said, "Go take a shower, dear. I'll bring dinner to your room in about fifteen minutes."

Maggie smiled wanly and said, "Thanks, Mom," then headed for her bedroom and a hot shower. The shower steamed away some of the stress and Maggie felt exhaustion taking over. She had just put her pajamas on when her mother showed up at the door with dinner on a tray.

Tears rolled down Maggie's cheeks and she said, "You didn't need to go to all this trouble."

"You've had quite a day," Estelle replied, "and this was the least I could do. Sit down, have your dinner then just to go to bed." Estelle set the tray on a small table next to a chair and left the room.

Maggie sat in the chair and looked at what her mother had fixed. There was a broiled chicken breast, some brown rice and mushrooms, carrots, and a homemade oatmeal cookie for dessert. She picked up the steaming cup of tea. The big gulp of tea told her, Estelle had laced it with whiskey. She had not realized how hungry she was until she began to eat. She thought to herself she needed to stop.

She finished her dinner and her tea and took the tray to the kitchen. She set it on the cupboard. Not seeing her mother, Maggie took her advice and headed straight to bed.

Morning came much too soon to Maggie's way of thinking. She crawled out of bed, dressed in her running outfit and took off out the back door. She was not surprised to find Sheriff Norton waiting for her.

"See you still have my back," she said with a smile.

"Yep, I can't have you not showing up for school."

They ran the rest of their run in silence, each deep in their own thoughts. At the end of the run, Sheriff Norton said, "Whatever happens, Maggie, I know you are doing your best."

Maggie nodded and finished by running the rest of the way home. She quickly showered, dressed and made herself a piece of toast. As she started out the door she remembered her car was still parked at work. She walked back in to pick up the phone as a car pulled into the driveway. She looked out to see Hope waiting for her.

As she got into the car she said, "How did you know I was just going to call you?"

"Sheriff Norton called me early this morning and said you'd need a ride and I should be here at this time."

"The man is a psychic."

Hope laughed and they made the short drive to the school.

Maggie was surprised to see Amy Walsh in the office. "Good morning, Amy. What has you here so early?"

"Well, Mrs. Parsons, I still need to meet your staff. They need to know I am truly a police officer and under my jacket I will carry a gun. The parents can believe I am your assistant, but the staff needs to be on board. They need to know I am undercover security and you are the person in charge."

"I hadn't thought about it. Hope, can you post a note on the work room door and let the teacher's know we are meeting this morning. I also need to brief them on everything we know about yesterday."

"No problem, I'll get right on it." Hope sat at her desk and fired up her computer. In minutes she had a large print notice to hang on the door.

As she left the office, Amy said, "You look all done in. I know this has been hard on you, but with Sheriff Norton in your corner we'll get to the bottom of this."

"I know. It's just so frustrating. I came home in the hopes of putting my life back together and now someone from my past is trying to tear it farther apart."

"I'll be in my official office until the meeting. Call if you need anything."

"Thanks again for doing this, Amy," Maggie said with a smile.

Amy left the office and Maggie went to her office to put the Mrs. Tea on. She could use a cup before the staff meeting. She wondered for not the first time how many children would not arrive today. She sat in her office thinking about what she needed to say to her staff. She listened as they entered the building. Many were talking in whispered tones. She wondered if they felt she was wrong for the position.

At 8:15 she started down to the work room. Hope made a reminder announcement at the same time. Maggie was surprised every teacher was already in the work room waiting for her.

"First, I want to thank all of you for your calm yesterday. In light of what happened, we were very lucky. I have learned from the Sheriff, whoever is behind this, knew me when I was a student here. This person for some reason wants to discredit me."

She paused then continued. "Yesterday some of you met, Amy Walsh. You were told she was an intern. I want you to know she is Officer Amy Walsh. She has been placed here by the Sheriff to give us an extra set of eyes."

Ida Waters spoke up, "Does that mean we're in danger?"

"Not in the least," Amy responded. "I am here at the request of the superintendent and Mrs. Parsons. Mrs. Parsons will handle all the school related things, just like she has been doing. I'm happy to give a stern lecture to any of your students who are being a bit mischievous, but my first job is to keep everyone safe. Sheriff Norton sees this as a threat to Mrs. Parsons and not the rest of the staff. As far as I know none of you has received notes from this person."

"While I appreciate the extra eyes, I'm not sure I like it," Ginny Barnes said timidly.

"None of us likes it, Ginny," responded Brett Anderson. "Let's hear everything Mrs. Parsons has to tell us before we start jumping to judgment."

"Thank you, Brett, for those kind words," Maggie said. "I want you to know Officer Walsh will be carrying a weapon under her jacket. She will not hesitate to take the appropriate measures should any of you or the children be in danger. If you have the Mitchell children, I don't expect them to be at school today. Please send a student to the office with your absences this morning, as I will need to know how many parents I have to call and reassure."

"Finally, the middle school and high school are sending their counselors to us in case any of your students are frightened or feel the need to talk to someone. I have not worked out with Hope where we are going to house them and it is entirely possible we will just let them walk the halls until noon and then send them back to their own buildings."

"Let them use my temporary office," offered Amy. "I need to be visible to the kids so they really think I am in training."

"Okay the office is where we will put them as there are two offices there. Does anyone have any other questions?"

Mrs. Feldstein stood, "Has Mr. Whitehead asked for my resignation yet?"

"Mrs. Feldstein, you did everything you were supposed to do, there is no reason to ask you to step down. I have spoken to Mr. Whitehead and it is not even an issue."

"Thank you."

"No, it is thanks to you we were able to get the Sheriff here so quickly and eventually find Jacob. If you had not reported it right away, and assumed he was just playing in the bathroom we would not have found the old tunnel leading to the shed. We have had maintenance in and the tunnel opening in the boys' restroom has been sealed. They also put a door and lock on the shed end of the tunnel. There is no way our mystery intruder will be able to get into the building and out unnoticed."

"I want all of you to try and relax. Enjoy your classes and have a good day." Maggie finished then waited as the staff filed out to see if anyone would want to talk to her privately. Seeing no one did, she made her way to the front doors, pasted a smile on her face and got ready to greet the children.

As the children came in Maggie spoke to them and felt things might turn out all right. She walked into the office behind the last of the children and said to Hope, "Each teacher is sending a child down with attendance today. I need to know how many are missing and out of which grades. I will have to report it to Mr. Whitehead as soon as we have the figures."

"It won't be a problem," Hope responded.

Maggie walked to her office and poured herself a cup of tea. She was dreading the call to her boss about attendance. This latest incident could well end her short lived career. She shrugged her shoulders and dug into some paperwork which needed to be completed.

Moments later she looked up as she heard a flurry of activity in the outer office. She walked out to see if she needed to step in.

"Oh, Maggie, you are just in time," Hope said with a smile this is Mrs. Wood, she is the grandmother of the Bright boys."

Maggie extended her hand and asked, "How is Caylee doing these days?"

"She be right fine, Miz Parsons. In fact she 'sisted I bring the boys to school today. Said they been out too long already."

"I'm glad to hear it," Maggie turned to the boys and asked, "Would you like me to walk you to class?"

The older boy said, "No, thanks. I know where my class is and I'll drop Micah off at his on the way."

"Good plan. Let Hope give you both a pass to class so, Ms. Walsh, the new assistant doesn't think you were playing around in the hallway."

With a smile on her face, Maggie returned to her office to finish up her paperwork and get ready for the call to Mr. Whitehead.

Ten minutes later, Hope showed up at her door. "You are not going to believe this!" she said excitedly.

"What now?" Maggie asked anxiously, her mind reeling with the possibility of impending doom.

"We have perfect attendance and the addition of the two Bright boys," Hope announced. "We even have all three Mitchell children here."

Maggie gasped. It was incredible. She reached her hand out for the attendance slips Hope held. Each one signed by the classroom teacher said, "Perfect." Maggie felt the tears running down her face. The parents believed in her. She had passed another hurdle.

"Are you alright? This is good news!" said Hope alarmed by the tears.

Maggie looked at her secretary and smiled, "These are tears of relief. It shows I have the confidence of all the parents. I hope it means we are past the worst."

The phone in the front office rang, "I'm off to get it. You call Mr. Whitehead."

Maggie nodded. She needed to get herself together before she called the superintendent. This might be the best call she had made to him yet.

Mr. Whitehead took Maggie's call and gave her compliments on the way she had handled the press yesterday. He seemed pleased to hear the school had perfect attendance and the two Bright children had decided it was time to come to school. The call was brief and left Maggie feeling as though she had missed an important message. She couldn't dwell on it. They were coming up to lunch time and she was determined to spend time on the playground and in the hallways. It was her job after all.

Maggie joined the first group of children in the cafeteria. She was immediately surrounded by children all wanting to share something with her. She took a moment to talk to each one. When things settled down she went to the teacher's workroom to see how things had gone this morning.

"Hi, Maggie is the count in?" said Ginny enthusiastically. "How was our attendance?"

"Perfect, not one student missing and both Bright boys have arrived."

Mrs. Feldstein looked up from her lunch and said, "It's wonderful. I admit to being surprised to see Jacob Mitchell this morning. He was the star."

"I'm sure he was," Maggie said smiling. "I was surprised they were here too. Hope said Matt Mitchell called and told her they wanted life to be normal."

"What nice people they are," Ida responded.

"Yes," said Maggie, "they are. I'll leave you to your lunches." She left the room and went toward the playground. It was time to make an appearance there before the next group went to lunch.

And so it went for Maggie until all three groups had been through lunch. She then went to her office.

Amy Walsh was there and asked for a minute of her time.

"Of course, come this way," she said as she headed for her office. "Would you care for a cup of tea?"

"No, but you go right ahead, and get some lunch while you are at it."

Maggie smiled as she followed Amy's request. "What did you need?"

"Sheriff Norton said both you and Mr. Mitchell mentioned someone named Aussie yesterday. He was wondering why you would?"

Maggie took a deep breath and a sip of tea then said, "Austin Howard was a classmate of ours. When he first came to Timberview he passed himself off as Australian, hence the nickname Aussie. He worked at the school in maintenance until sometime last year."

"Would it be the same Austin Howard who vandalized the school just before it opened?"

"Yes," Maggie said sadly, "I'm afraid we were very unkind to him when we found out we'd been duped. I dumped him as a boyfriend and we pretty much shut him out of our activities our senior year of high school. Back then it didn't seem so cruel, but I never thought he'd hold a grudge for twenty years."

"Well, it seems Mr. Howard isn't the only one with a grudge," Amy replied.

Startled Maggie said, "What do you mean? Who else has a grudge?"

"I don't know, but Austin Howard has been in the county jail since the school break-in, he couldn't possibly be responsible for the things going on here."

"But Jacob said the person went to school with me and he had worked here. I cannot think of anyone else who would do such a thing."

"Sheriff Norton will need to know this; I'll call him and get him looking for classmates of yours."

"Have him call Erika Estwick of E and E Investigations. She's been looking into my classmates for me on a personal matter. I'll call her and tell her to expect the Sheriff to call."

"Thanks, Maggie, now eat your lunch," Amy said with a smile as she left the office.

While Maggie ate her lunch, she pondered who else could have hated her so much. Who hated her enough to put the children in harm's way? Why not just confront her and be done with it? She hoped the Sheriff and Erika could figure it out.

She reached for the phone to dial Erika's number.

"E and E Investigations, how may I help you?"

"Is Erika Estwick in?"

"She is. May I tell her whose calling?"

"Yes, this is Maggie Parsons."

"One moment please."

Maggie thought this was not the person who answered the phone the last time she called.

"Maggie, this is Erika, has something come up?"

"Yes, it seems someone besides Austin Howard has it in for me. I'm sure you heard the news about Jacob Mitchell disappearing yesterday."

"I did hear it. I understand he is home."

"Yes, and he said the man who took him went to school with me and he worked at the school. Matt and I both assumed it was Austin Howard, but he's been in jail since he vandalized the school. Anyway, the Sheriff wants to call you and compare notes, I said I'd call ahead and let you know it's okay with me."

"Thanks for the heads up. I was going to call you today anyway. Maybe after I talk with your Sheriff we should all three sit down and talk. I have plenty to tell you and Austin Howard is a big part of it."

"Okay. Where would you like to meet?"

"I'll call you after I talk to the Sheriff. Are you still at your mother's?"

"Yes, I'm still there until the week-end."

"Okay, I'll call you later. Thanks again for giving me the call."

Maggie set the phone back in its cradle wondering what had come up now. She also wondered if she really wanted to know. She shook her head, finished her lunch and went back to work. She still had a job to attend to.

Maggie ended her day much as she started it, standing in front of the building watching the children get onto their buses. She was happy to see it end. She walked back to her office to finish up anything left undone before going home.

Once home, Maggie went straight to her room and took a shower. She changed into a pair of white slacks and a pale blue blouse. All she had to do was slip on sandals and she would be ready for whatever the Sheriff and Erika Estwick could throw at her. She went to the kitchen to get a cup of tea and see what plans her mother had for the evening.

On the counter was one of her mom's famous notes. It read:

Maggie,

I have gone to dine with Dr Gordon. Please do not wait up. There is tuna noodle salad in the fridge and I'm sure you can find lunch meat for a sandwich.

Love,
Mother
xoxox

Maggie chuckled and made her tea. It might be better if her mom were not here for this particular meeting. She was most likely not going to want to hear some of the things being said. Then on the other hand her mom was one who liked to know all the gossip first. Maggie shrugged and continued making her tea.

She took her cup of tea to the living room, and curled up with a book she was trying to read. All she could do now was to wait for Erika's call.

When the phone rang, Maggie jumped, she'd been so engrossed in her book it took her a minute to identify the sound. She quickly picked up the phone and said hello.

"Maggie, this is Erika. The Sheriff and I have compared notes. We'd like to come and talk to you."

"I'm at my mother's and she is out so I will be waiting."

"Have you had dinner?"

"No, I was just reading a book and waiting for you."

"Good, the Sheriff has made arrangements for dinner to be delivered. We'll be there in about fifteen minutes."

Maggie hung up the phone and went to the kitchen. The least she could do was make coffee. She checked to see if there were any soft drinks in the refrigerator and was surprised to see her mom had coke and sprite chilling. She got down glasses and cups not knowing what either of her guests would be drinking. She had to be doing something or she'd find herself pacing the kitchen.

In no time, Erika and Terry showed up, each driving separately. A catering truck followed them. Maggie opened the door surprised to see a catering truck.

"I thought maybe you had ordered pizza," she said.

"I would have," Erika answered as she entered, "but Mr. Big Bucks there said we needed to have nourishing food. I think he's ordered enough for an army."

Terry Norton smiled as he led the caterers into the kitchen. "If you just set things on the counter, I think we can manage."

Once the caterers left, he opened each covered container and told the ladies to dig in.

"Where did you order this from?" Maggie asked.

"Remember the quiet little restaurant I took you to?"

She nodded as she helped herself to some spinach salad.

"Well, they cater too, so I thought I'd treat us to a nice dinner before we get down to business."

"Works for me," Erika said as she settled at the dining room table.

"I have coke, sprite, or coffee," Maggie offered her guests.

"Ah, but I have red and white wine," the Sheriff said with a wink.

"I'm guessing you are off duty."

"Most definitely, I don't usually get to dine with two beautiful women so I'm making the most of it." He joined the ladies at the dining room table and they made small talk while they ate. The Sheriff had picked out two pasta dishes, some beef tips in gravy, and some shrimp cocktail. When the meal was over, the three of them cleaned up.

"You don't have to wash the caterer's pans. He will pick them up from here in about an hour," the Sheriff said. "I didn't want to make any extra work. Besides, they are bringing dessert."

Erika groaned.

Maggie laughed, "Like I saved room for dessert."

"It's why they aren't coming for an hour."

They retreated to the living room with wine glasses. Maggie sat in her father's chair, leaving Erika in her mother's straight back chair and Terry on the sofa.

"Ok, I guess it's time we get down to business," Erika started pulling some papers out of her brief case. "I took the liberty of having my report typed in triplicate. I have a copy for each of you." She handed papers to both of them. "As we go through this, I am going to tell you why each person could be a suspect and why I have ruled them out. Feel free to ask questions or give comments as I go."

"Maggie, I started with you," she said as a matter-of-fact. "All incidents seem to have started after you arrived. As I did my research I found there to be no reason to suspect you of staging any of this. You are still mourning the loss of your family and chose to dig into your job as a way of dealing with the loss."

"It gels with what I have learned," added the Sheriff.

"After I started looking at your friends from high school. I started with those who never left. Which brings us to Austin Howard. He never left Timberview. He married; his wife had several miscarriages and then died from ovarian cancer. He worked in maintenance for the school until last spring. He was fired just weeks before the accident killed your family. While I cannot connect him to it at this time, I have not ruled him out as part of it. He was released from jail four days after the vandalism at the school, so he could be the person behind the opening in the fence and the kidnapping of Jacob Mitchell. I am continuing to look into him as a person of interest."

"My office has put him under surveillance although it might be a little too late to catch him at anything," added the Sheriff.

"I thought Officer Walsh said he was still in jail."

"He did spend another night there. He was picked up for drunk and disorderly about three days ago. He was released the next morning after he slept it off."

"Glen Swift returned in the wake of his father's sudden death. It was excellent timing for Glen as he had been out of work for six months and his unemployment was running out. They were able to sell their home before the housing market took a tumble and he has lived here running the grocery for the past two years. I see no reason to put him on a suspect list; however there was something shady about the way he lost his job."

"Do you know what i5 was?" the Sheriff asked?

"Yes, but it involves someone else on the list. I'd like to hold that part until we get there."

The Sheriff looked at Maggie, "Is it okay with you?"

"It's fine as long as I get to hear the problem at some point. It's also nice to know Glen is not a suspect. He was very supportive at the parent meeting I had."

"Good, since we are done with Glen let's move on," Erika said as she began on the next person. "Matt Mitchell was laid-off from his job, again under shady circumstances. He moved home because his dad offered to retire and turn the lumber business over him. He has been here running the business for about a year. He sold his house, but had to sell at a lower value than he wanted. He was able to avoid losing the house. He is not a suspect and I see no further reason to investigate him."

"I know of nothing which would cause me to look at Matt Mitchell for any of this," agreed the Sheriff.

Just then, there was a knock on the kitchen door. "It will be the caterers," said the Sheriff slyly. "Don't say anything important until I get back." He left the room to answer the door.

Maggie decided on small talk, "Erika, may I ask how you got into the investigation business?"

Relieved to have a different topic, Erika replied, "My dad was Edward Estwick of Estwick Investigations. When I was a little girl he used to take me with him on the easy jobs. I loved it. So, in college I studied criminal justice, and forensic science. When I graduated, he changed the name to E and E Investigations. We worked as a team until he died three years ago. Now it's just me, but I feel like he is with me most days so I haven't changed the name."

"Wow, some story. He must have been an exciting man."

"I thought so, he was my hero."

"Ta-da," said the Sheriff from the doorway. In his hand he had balanced three slices of volcano chocolate cake with vanilla ice cream on the side.

Both women stood to take a piece from him. He left the room and returned moments later with three steaming cups of coffee.

"Not to worry, Maggie, there is plenty of this left for your mother," he said winking.

Maggie rolled her eyes as she stuck her spoon into the chocolate delight. After her first bite she let out a big sigh.

"My thoughts exactly," Erika chimed in. "How did you think of this?"

"I heard from a little bird it was a favorite. So, since I was buying dinner I ordered this, too."

"Many many thanks," Maggie mumbled over a mouthful.

The Sheriff nodded and continued eating his. Erika was oblivious to either one of them; she was so immersed in the chocolate delight. Finally when everyone was done, the Sheriff collected the plates and took them to the kitchen. The women heard the water running as he rinsed the plates and set them in the dishwasher with the rest of the dinner dishes. He found the soap under the sink and set the dishwasher in motion before returning to the living room.

"Ok," Maggie said, "we need to get back to the issue at hand. So far the way I see it, two of my classmates have lost jobs under suspicious circumstances, but neither of them have any reason to lodge a campaign against me or the school. Do I have it so far?"

"Sounds about right," the Sheriff agreed.

"Next on the list you gave to me is Ashton (Blake) Blythe. She has recently returned home in the wake of a nasty divorce. It seems her wealthy husband was not so wonderful and his mistress pressed him for a divorce. After about six months he gave into her and filed for divorce giving Ashton sole custody of their two children and a lump sum pay off in the seven figure category. Ashton was devastated at first, but began to see this as her way of leaving a loveless marriage and still keeping her kids. She has no reason I can find to want to get at Maggie or the school. I have removed her from the suspect list."

"This mistress must hold some real power," Maggie concluded.

"We'll get to her as she seems to play a huge role in all of this," Erika replied. "The last person on Maggie's list of close friends is Laura Gilbert."

"But Laura isn't here," Maggie said. "She hasn't been here since we started college."

"I understand, Maggie, however; I did look into everyone connected to you and Laura is a bigger connection than you know. We will start with college. Laura went to a different college than you or Ashton. Things went well for her the first year and she found herself with a summer job and a steady beau. His name was Austin Howard."

"No way!" exclaimed Maggie, "she was as angry at Aussie as the rest of us."

"Well he spent the summer with her and at her homecoming dance she asked him if he'd like to settle down and have children. Austin being true to his character laughed at her and told her maybe in his next life. She got angry and sent him away, refused his calls and had him escorted away from her dorm by campus police. She then moved away for the second semester. She returned for the summer semester and lived with her mother in a little off campus house. She kept to herself, did not date and graduated magna cum laude and second in her class. She has moved from place to place creating wonderful antique galleries wherever she goes. Her daughter Ashton Margaret was born during her second semester. From the time she was old enough to enter school she has lived in boarding schools in the east, vacationing in exotic places with her beautiful mother. She is currently starting her junior year in an exclusive girls' college in the east."

"How does it fit in with anything other than to suggest Aussie might be the child's father?" Maggie demanded.

"If you remember, Laura was the mistress of one of your husband's partners. Laura was ruled out as an accomplice, but could have been very instrumental in the death of your family."

Maggie gasped. "There is no way Laura would have hurt my family. She had no reason to even know them."

"Well, you are wrong. Laura has had on retainer a high priced investigator for years. He has kept track of everything you and your classmates have been up to. It seems Laura was involved with Glen's boss at the time he was laid-off. She was helping him to downsize. We feel pretty certain it was her idea for Glen be on the chopping block. Then there was Matt Mitchell. His boss was going into a realignment of assets in the hopes of staving off bankruptcy. When we looked into his finances it seems he'd been dipping into company funds to keep his mistress happy. And who might his mistress have been? Yes, our Laura. She seems to get around. Each of the men she is involved with has ties to someone in your class. Care to guess whose mistress she is right now?"

Maggie shook her head to try and clear it. She was unable to take all of this in. Why would Laura want to get back at all of them? Finally when she could find her voice she said, "What is her purpose for wanting to hurt all of us?"

"It seems she has been plotting her revenge since she was scorned for becoming pregnant."

"But why, she had to know Ashton and I had no idea."

"It seems both of your mothers' kept sending her hush money after their initial letter. She thought of it as a pay off from you and Ashton. She's been trying to get revenge all these years."

"Does Aussie even know he has a daughter?"

"Yes, it is what Laura holds over his head to get him to do her dirty work. She has sent him photos, but will not tell him where Ashton Margaret is, nor has she told her daughter who her father is. Which is how she got him to vandalize the school, your car, cut the fence and we think kidnap Jacob Mitchell. Austin's downfall is he cannot hurt anyone."

"So, how do we go about catching her?" Maggie wanted to know?"

"The Sheriff and I are working on it. We needed to bring you up to speed. Then we need to meet with your classmates and bring them up to speed. At this point, we feel all of you are in danger. No one knows what her next attack might be. So far she has her sights set on getting you fired."

"This is incredible, like something on a bad TV show," Maggie said, "How did things come to this? Why didn't she try to contact us after college? It seems she knew where all of us were."

"Revenge is a dangerous thing. I don't believe she can see beyond her hatred. It has made her a very determined and demented person. She is no longer the person you hung out with as a teen. I see her to be dangerous."

"What am I supposed to do?"

"We have several ideas on what you should do. If you plan to continue running in the morning, do not leave the house until the Sheriff arrives. He can keep you covered during by running with you. We don't think she'll do anything while he is around. You have Amy Walsh while you are at work, so we feel you will be safe there."

"This is nuts! I cannot take this all in. I need some time to think. It's like stepping into some freaky time warp."

"Let's start with those two things. Now, can you set up a meeting with your friends?"

"How soon do you want it? Where do you want it? What are we going to do with their children?"

The Sheriff spoke up at this point, "Why don't you have Hope set up the meeting for tomorrow after school. They can come to the school and I'll have a couple of off duty officers with things to do with the kids in your gym."

"Okay, do you want me to call Hope tonight?"

"No, just wait and have her call first thing in the morning."

"I can do it. What about my mother? Is she safe?"

"I don't know," Erika said honestly.

"I took the lead on this and let your brother and Doctor Gordon in on things. It is why she has been gone so long tonight. Doctor Gordon is proposing to her....try to act surprised in the morning when she tells you. Your brother said he will be on the look-out, but I have extra patrols in his neighborhood for the time being," the Sheriff responded.

"Oh my, this is just too much to fast," Maggie said with another shake to her head. She felt like she was in some kind of freak show. This couldn't be happening. Things were too mixed up, too out of control.

Erika stood, "Maggie, you go to bed. We have everything under control at the moment. Just remember not to run before the Sheriff arrives and to set the meeting for tomorrow night. In the meantime, get some rest." She picked up her briefcase and made her way to the back door.

"That's it?" Maggie asked, "You two spring all this on me and then just leave? What am I supposed to do? How do you possibly think I'll be able to sleep?"

"I'll make us a second cup of coffee and hang around for a bit. Then I can try to answer some of your questions," the Sheriff responded as he headed toward the kitchen.

Maggie sank into her father's chair seeking comfort, but was unable to recapture the safe feeling she'd always felt when sitting there. Her head was spinning. Why would Laura do this? What had she ever done? They had been friends since childhood. She, Ashton, and Laura had been their own brand of the 'Three Stooges.' How had it come to this? Better yet, why was she the last one to know?

The Sheriff returned and handed Maggie a cup of coffee, "What question would you like answered first?"

Maggie took a sip of the coffee, and then said, "Why is Laura so spiteful? She was not like this when we were kids. I don't understand."

"Let me put it this way. In her mind, you and Ashton, her best friends in the world deserted her when she needed you both. Not only did you leave her in the cold, you did it in the same way you had turned on Austin Howard, the father of her unborn child. So, she has been hurt and angry since she was nineteen years old. It is a long time to let hurt and anger fester."

"I'm with you to a point. Why if she was so angry with us, did she name her daughter after us?"

"I think she was trying to remind herself of the anger and betrayal. She has never spent much time with her daughter since her daughter turned five and entered school. Laura sent her away. The only vacations she took with her daughter were in exotic places where they were not likely to run into anyone she had known growing up."

"What about Laura's mom in all this? She couldn't have been happy."

"It seems her mother has a house close to the boarding school Ashton Margaret attended. The girl spent all school holidays and occasional week-ends with her very loving grandmother."

"At least she has known love in her life."

"She has become more and more curious about her mother's childhood. She recently learned she was named for her mother's two best friends and has asked to meet you. Laura has forbidden it, saying she does not know where either of you are. Something we know is a lie."

"Why has she become a mistress to so many men? Didn't she ever find someone who would love her and marry her? Did she not ever think about having more children?"

"It seems she has never really gotten over Austin Howard which is part of what she holds over him. She sent a sympathy card every time Austin and his wife lost a child. She never let him forget, he threw away a child and a life with her. Each man she was with bestowed on her lavish gifts of jewelry. She also found a way to get each of them to provide for her for six months after their arrangement was over. She banked the money. She is a very shrewd business woman. She has sold each of her antique galleries for small fortunes and has invested her money wisely, always leaving enough to open another gallery."

"By killing my husband and children, what did she hope to gain? Didn't it destroy me enough? Now she wants to take my livelihood?"

"I told you she has gone over the edge. She is no longer thinking rationally. She has not been able to discredit you and I am afraid she will begin personal attacks on you and those you love. It's why I put all this protection in place for your family."

Maggie nodded. She was beginning to feel very sleepy. Maybe things were finally setting in.

The Sheriff reached for her cup as it slipped from her hand. He set the cup on the end table and picked Maggie up and carried her to her bed room. He deftly pulled back the covers on her bed and laid her in it. He covered her and walked from the room. He picked up the two cups and carried them to the kitchen. The little bit of sleeping powder Dr. Gordon had given him worked. He rinsed the cups, turned off the coffee maker, turned out the lights, locked the door and let himself out. He had a pillow and blanket in his truck. He would park himself where he could see the house and keep watch. He expected little sleep this night.

Maggie had a fitful night. She awoke to the sound of voices coming from the kitchen. She was surprised to find herself still dressed as she had been when the Sheriff and Erika had been here. She tried to think. The last thing she remembered was talking to the Sheriff about Laura and feeling tired. He must have put something in the coffee so she could sleep. Well. it wasn't going to happen again.

She leapt from her bed, headed straight for her closet, pulled out her running clothes and quickly threw them on. No one was going to dictate to her when she could and couldn't run.

She stopped dead in her tracks when she got to the kitchen and found the Sheriff in his running clothes sitting at the counter sharing a cup of coffee with her mother.

"We need to talk," she said through her teeth to the Sheriff as she headed for the back door.

"Maggie, mind your manners," her mother admonished.

"Not now, Mother, this is between Sheriff Norton and me. We have some things we need to get settled." She stormed out the door.

"Well..." Estelle started.

"It's okay, Mrs. Mills, I have this tongue lashing coming," he chuckled as he followed Maggie out the door. She was a block and a half ahead of him so he sprinted to catch up with her. When he finally caught her he asked breathlessly, "Do you plan to continue at this pace? I cannot possibly talk to you and keep this pace."

She stopped and looked him squarely in the eye, "What is the meaning of drugging me last night? Did you think I was so fragile everything you shared with me would make me fall apart?"

"No, I just wanted to be sure you would get some sleep."

"How did you know the drug you gave me wouldn't hurt me?"

"I got it from Dr. Gordon when I talked to him yesterday. Are we still going to run or are we going to stand here and argue?"

"Arrgh!" was all the response he got as Maggie started jogging down the path. "This is not over."

"Some how I didn't think it would be. By the way, your mother invited me for breakfast. She has some news to share with you."

"What are you talking about? Does Mom know what is going on?"

"Not unless Dr. Gordon told her. I don't think he did as, she didn't let on this morning."

They continued their run in silence. Maggie headed straight to the shower when they arrived back at her mother's. Fifteen minutes later she was dressed and ready for work. She joined her mother and the Sheriff in the kitchen, ate very little and was completely surprised when her mother showed off her engagement ring from Dr. Gordon.

Maggie and the Sheriff left, Maggie to head for the school and the Sheriff to head home for a shower and change of clothes.

Sleeping in the car had not been the most delightful thing the Sheriff had done recently, but at least Maggie had been safe. He'd done his job last night and felt Maggie would be safe because Amy Walsh would be in the school building.

Maggie arrived at the school and made a swift look around the parking lot before getting out of her car. She felt foolish, because so far no one had tried to harm her, but she knew she would be much more cautious until this was over. She went immediately to her office and started locating the phone numbers she would be calling in a few minutes. She started a pot of tea and sat at her desk trying to decide what she would say and who she would call first.

Hope found her sitting at her desk looking forlorn a few minutes later when she came in to start her day. She quietly poured Maggie a cup of tea and asked, "Would you like me to make the calls?"

Maggie looked up and shook her head, "This is something I have to do. Somehow I feel I am partly to blame for all of this, whatever this is."

"You have done nothing to bring any of this on," Hope assured her. "You are a victim just like the people you are going to call. They can be thankful they've not lost their families."

Maggie took a sip of her tea. She looked at Hope and said, "Thanks for putting it in perspective for me. Will you run interference with the staff this morning?"

"Not a problem," Hope replied cheerily as she left closing Maggie's door behind her.

Maggie picked up the phone and dialed the first number on her list.

"Hello."

"Mrs. Mitchell, this is Maggie Parsons, is Matt still there?"

"He sure is, but I know the kids are still here so it can't be they're in any trouble yet," she replied.

"No, this has to do with Jacob's disappearance."

"I'll get him right away."

"Hi, Maggie, what's up?" Matt asked.

"Can you and your wife meet here at the school as soon as school gets out today? The Sheriff has some information. I can have the kids stay. I have taken care of all daycare needs right here at the school."

"We'll be there."

"Great I look forward to seeing you both."

Maggie set the phone back in its cradle. She felt as though she'd deceived Matt. There was so much she'd left out. She couldn't dwell on it now; she had two more calls to make. She picked up the phone and dialed the number for Glen Swift praying Glen would answer the phone, knowing how possessive his wife was.

"Swifts, Glen speaking."

"Hi, Glen, this is Maggie Parsons. Could you and your wife come to a meeting after school today?"

"What kind of trouble have the boys gotten into this time?"

"Oh no, nothing about the boys, this has to do with the incidents happening at the school. The Sheriff has some information. I've taken care of daycare right here at the school so, if you and your wife could come as soon as school gets out we can get you informed and on your way."

"Count us in."

"Thanks, Glen, see you this afternoon."

Maggie was thinking this had been too easy. She still had to call Ashton. Hopefully this would go as well.

"Hello."

"Hi, Mrs. Blake, this is Maggie Parsons, is Ashton available?"

"Yes, she is. One moment please."

Maggie heard her gently set the phone down and heard her walking away.

"Hi, Mags, what ya want?" Ashton asked, using her childhood nickname for Maggie.

"I need to know if you can come to a meeting at the school at the end of the day."

"Sure I think I can get mom to watch my son."

"Good I'll have your daughter stay. I'm providing day-care here during the meeting. I'll see you at the end of the day."

"I'll be there, but what aren't you telling me?"

"Nothing, the Sheriff asked me to call some of the parents in so he can give them information about what's been going on at the school."

"Oh, okay. I'll see you later."

Maggie hung up the phone feeling like she lied to her friends. She hadn't really; she just did not given them all the information she had. She decided she couldn't dwell on it as she had her job to do. She stepped from behind her desk and headed to the front office.

"Everything okay this morning, Hope?"

"Yes, Amy Walsh did your morning walkthrough and talked with all the staff. She told them you were working on something for the Sheriff. They seemed okay with it."

"Good," Maggie said as she plastered a smile on her face and went out to greet the children. She found her smile became less forced as the children stopped for hugs or to give her a high five on their way into the building. She walked into the building with the Smith boys and started making her own rounds, looking for stray children or any problems which might be arising.

As she entered the fourth and fifth wing of the building she saw Amy Walsh coming toward her.

"Thank you for making rounds this morning."

"No problem. If I am going to be your assistant I should act like one. I thought the staff would feel better about me if I spent some time with them. They are good people."

"I would agree with you. Thanks again anyway."

Both women made their way down different hallways. Amy to the temporary office she had and Maggie toward the kitchen. She needed to make arrangement for snacks for the kids after school.

"Mrs. Olsen," Maggie called as she entered the kitchen. Fans were blowing moving the warm air around. Getting no answer, she walked farther into the kitchen and called again, "Mrs. Olsen."

Maggie heard a door slam and walked toward the sound. She almost collided with Mrs. Olsen who had her arms full of food containers for the day's lunch.

"Oh, Mrs. Parsons, I'm so sorry I didn't hear you. I was in the cooler."

"It's my fault, Mrs. Olsen, let me help you."

"What brings you to the kitchen?"

"I need some simple snacks for about six kids this afternoon. Can you do something for me?"

"Sure I can put some fruit snacks, crackers and cheese or peanut butter, and some fruit drinks together. Is there anything else?"

"No, Mrs. Olsen, I'll let you get back to work. Thank you."

"My pleasure."

Maggie took a deep breath as she left the kitchen. Smelled like apple cobbler. She hoped she'd be able to get some later. Mrs. Olsen arrived about 6 a.m. every morning and started baking. She was a one woman cooking machine. She turned out some of the best meals Maggie had ever tasted in a school. She made her way back to her office to do some much neglected paper work.

Hope entered Maggie's office quietly at 11 a. m. She carried a dish with Mrs. Olsen's apple cobbler in it. She knew it was one of Maggie's favorites.

Maggie looked up as Hope came in. She could smell the warm cobbler Hope carried. "Am I starting lunch with dessert today?"

"You might as well, and then be sure you do eat your lunch. It will free you up to spend time in the cafeteria and on the playground without missing your own lunch."

"Well thank you for this," Maggie said pointing to the apple cobbler sitting on her desk.

"All part of the service," Hope replied. "Are you still planning to move this weekend?"

"Yes, my brother and Sheriff Norton are bringing their trucks and I have a U-haul trailer so we should be able to move most of the big stuff. I'm leaving some there so the house can be staged for an open house."

"Good, I'm glad none of this has changed your plans."

"No, my Mom got engaged last night. I really need to move into a place of my own."

"That's great! I wish her all the best."

"Me, too."

"I'll leave you now; don't forget to eat your lunch." Hope left the office and closed the door gently.

Maggie smiled it looked like lunch was starting with dessert after all. She picked up the still warm cobbler and put her spoon in. It was just as heavenly as she'd expected. After finishing her lunch, Maggie made her way to the cafeteria for the first lunch group. She spent time with them and then made her way to the playground to see the other group out there. She did this with all three groups before heading in to the kindergarten classes where she was to read *If You Give a Mouse a Cookie*. After reading the children made their own cookies by putting frosting on sugar cookies provided by Mrs. Olsen. Maggie was delighted when one child offered her a cookie with too much frosting on it. She took the cookie, said thank you, and enjoyed every single bite of it.

She returned to the office. Hope told her there were no messages and she prepared herself to send the children on home. As she stepped outside she found herself again searching the area looking for something out of place. She took in the Sheriff's car at the far end of the parking lot. It made her feel safer to see his car there. The bell rang and the children came out with their teachers heading for their busses. A few children stopped to hug Maggie. She noticed the Mitchells, Swifts, and Ashton arriving and going inside as the kids were boarding the busses. As the last bus rolled off the lot Maggie headed for the library.

When the Sheriff saw Maggie enter the library and take a seat in the back he began, "First I want to thank you all for coming on such short notice. I have some things to tell you which go back a few years and lead up to now. It might not make much sense in bits and pieces, but it's the only way I know how to tell you. Glen, do you remember anything strange about when you lost your job?"

"No, just got told they were downsizing. They gave me a month of pay and I drew unemployment."

"Did you find it strange it they were keeping people with less seniority than you had?"

"Don't remember giving it much thought. I was more worried about finding a job and keeping my family together."

"Well it seems your boss had a mistress at the time who gave him your name as a person to eliminate."

"How does it make sense? I rarely saw the boss and have no idea who his girlfriend might have been. We didn't socialize with the upper management, just the guys in the neighborhood and the guys in my unit at the shop."

"Be that as it may, someone you knew had a hand in getting you laid off."

"Maybe I can make more sense," Maggie suggested as she stood up. They all turned to where she was standing.

"When we were in high school, we all hung out together. We also included Austin Howard and Laura Gilbert in our group. When Laura was in her second year of college she got pregnant. Apparently she contacted my mom and Ashton's. Instead of telling us, they took it upon themselves to tell her Ashton and I wanted nothing to do with her. They sent her some money with the letter. They also continued to send money to her afterward for about six months. She has taken it into her head we were shutting her out the way we shut Aussie out years ago. She thought because she was having Aussie's child we had turned on her. She has a daughter named Ashton Margaret who is attending an all girls' college in the east. She has never allowed her daughter to meet Aussie. She has become an astute business woman, opening and selling several successful antique galleries. She has also set herself up as a mistress to wealthy business owners who in turn have made her wealthy. Each of these business men has had something to do with each of us and has had an impact on our lives as a result."

"So you are saying my losing my job is because of some desire for revenge Laura has?" Matt asked.

The Sheriff answered, "It would seem so. So far the only one who has lost family members is Maggie."

Ashton gasped, "You mean Laura had something to do with the death of your family? I cannot believe it."

"I'm having trouble getting my head around this, too," Maggie admitted.

"This is what I have done to ensure your safety. There are extra patrols in each of your neighborhoods. I have an undercover police officer in the school building. Still I need you to be aware of your surroundings at all times."

"Wait, wait," Ashton cried. "I am still trying to get my mind around all of this." She looked at the Sheriff and then at Maggie and asked, "Does this mean my husband's mistress is Laura?"

"I'm so sorry, Ashton," Maggie said, "It looks like she is."

Ashton sobbed. Maggie went to her and put her arm around Ashton's shoulders.

"Sheriff, what can we do?" Matt asked. "I know I want my family's safe. If taking Jacob was a hint as to what we can expect I want her brought to justice."

"We all do, Matt. I am working on where she is at the moment. So far, we are unable to locate her," the Sheriff said. "Just be aware of everything around you. Know where your children are and who they are with. Don't go anyplace alone."

Mrs. Swift spoke up, "Why are my husband and Matt being targeted? They didn't know anything about all of this?"

"In her mind, this is what happened in high school to Austin Howard. She is angry, hurt, and no longer thinking like a logical adult. She's lived for revenge for nineteen years. It's become an obsession with her. She's crossed the fine line to insanity," the Sheriff said. "I cannot stress how dangerous she can become. Maggie knows firsthand how deadly she can be."

Everyone turned again to look at Maggie. She looked at each one in turn and said, "I did not know Laura was behind the deaths of my husband and children until last night. I have not been keeping anything from you. I would not knowingly put you or your families in any danger."

Matt spoke first, "We know, Maggie. We are just trying to understand how this all happened and how we can make it stop."

"I know," she said softly, "me, too."

They quietly left the meeting and went to pick up their children. Maggie did her walk through the building and was surprised to find the Sheriff waiting in her office when she returned.

"Well, that went over like the proverbial lead balloon," she said as she went to her desk to retrieve her purse and keys.

"They are as shell shocked as you were last night. Give it some time."

They walked out of the office and toward the parking lot. Maggie was quiet until she reached her car.

"Terry, do you have a plan to catch Laura?" she asked.

"I'm working on one as fast as I can," he answered.

"Thank you." She got into her car and drove home.

Terry Norton watched as Maggie drove out of the school driveway and turned toward home. He hoped he had a plan. At this point he had a twenty-four hour tail on Austin Howard. He'd called a friend at the FBI and they were trying to trace Laura Gilbert. She had gone underground somewhere. He knew she was lurking around waiting to strike again.

All the players here in Timberview had been warned. He could only hope they would be diligent in watching their surroundings. He was hopeful.

What was his big plan? How was he going to protect three families and Maggie? How was he going to keep the school children safe? He hated when children were involved. People who used children as pawns to further their demented causes made him angry. Children were sacred, to be cared for and loved. His humble was his opinion anyway.

He moved to Timberview because he didn't like the abuse cases that had crossed his desk in the city. He thought moving here; he'd see fewer cases of child abuse and neglect. So far he'd been right. Now if he could just figure out what Laura Gilbert had planned he could stop it before anyone got hurt.

Being Sheriff in a small town was no certainty he'd be getting a good night's sleep. Terry Norton made his way home and brewed a pot of coffee. He found a frozen dinner in his freezer and popped it in the microwave. He thumbed through the mail he'd picked up on the way in bills and more bills, nothing that wouldn't wait. The buzzer on the microwave went off. He took the turkey dinner out and set it on the counter to cool. He opened the cupboard and took out a cup. He poured himself a cup of coffee and took his makeshift dinner to the table. While eating he continued to mull over what he knew about the Laura Gilbert situation.

Much of what he learned had come from Erika Estwick. She was a thorough investigator. He hoped she'd come up with some more. Maybe he'd call her in the morning and get her take on the whole thing. She might have a different perspective.

The day behind him, he made his way to his in home gym. He hadn't needed a three bedroom house, but could see the advantage now. He'd turned one of the bedrooms into a home gym. He was able to work out daily in the privacy of his own home. After his workout he showered and plopped down on the sofa to watch TV. Which is where he fell asleep.

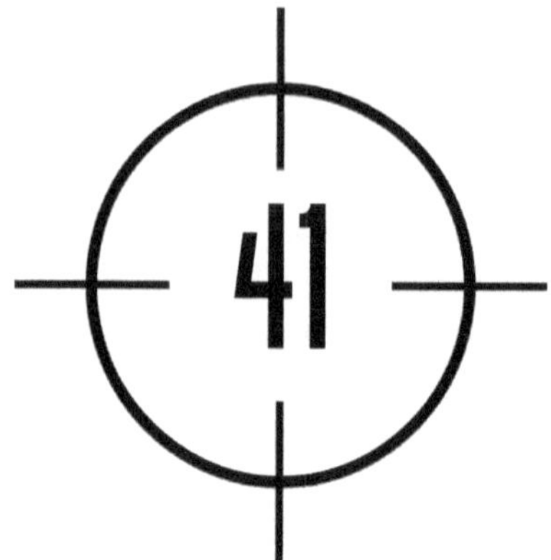

Maggie made her way home after the meeting. She could still see the looks on the faces of her friends.

They were shocked and disbelieving. Now she had to face her mother and tell her, they could be in danger. She was not looking forward to it and was pleased to see Dr. Gordon's car parked out front when she pulled in the driveway.

"Hello, Maggie," her mother said cheerfully as Maggie came through the back door. "Dr. Gordon is going to join us for dinner."

"Great! I have something I need to talk to you about and I'd like Dr. Gordon to hear it."

"Sounds serious," her mother said looking up from the salad she was making.

"It is, but it can wait until after we eat." Maggie got busy setting the table for dinner.

Dr. Gordon came in from the living room. He took in the scene of Estelle in the kitchen and Maggie setting the table. Estelle was looking perplexed and Maggie looked worn out. He decided it was time to jump in, "How are you, Maggie?"

"I'm fine, Dr. Gordon. I've been meaning to call and tell you the sleep medication has worked well."

"I'm glad to hear it. You looked tired today, is there anything I can help with?"

"I don't think so," she replied. "Mom, is dinner about ready to be put on the table?"

"It is," Estelle replied, "you two just sit down and I'll bring everything."

The meal was a quiet affair. Congratulations to the newly engaged couple and other inane small talk. At the end of the meal Maggie offered to do dishes and bring coffee to the living room. She had something she wanted to share with both of them.

In the living room Estelle and Dr. Gordon waited for Maggie to join them. She entered carrying a tray of coffee, cream and sugar. She was surprised to see her mother seated next to Dr. Gordon on the sofa. Her mother rarely sat anywhere other than her straight back chair.

"So, Maggie," Dr. Gordon began, "what is this news you have for us? It sounded serious."

"It is," Maggie replied, "There have been some discoveries in the school problems."

"Well, I would think it would be good news," commented Estelle.

"I wish I could say it was," Maggie responded. "It seems all of the problems at the school go back to Laura Gilbert and her pregnancy. She even arranged for Glen Swift and Matt Mitchell to lose their jobs. She is directly responsible for Ashton's divorce."

"How can this be?" Estelle asked in astonishment.

"It seems they can even trace her to a connection with the death of Ben and the children," Maggie said softly.

Estelle gasped.

Dr. Gordon put his arm around Estelle and asked, "If this is true, are we in danger?"

"Yes, it would seem so."

"What can we do? I have no intention of being a sitting duck," Estelle said.

"In the meeting tonight the Sheriff told us we need to be aware of our surroundings at all times. He also said we should not go anyplace alone. They have extra patrols in our area, but they cannot be here all the time."

"I suppose this means you will have to stop running." Estelle stated.

"No, Sheriff Norton will be here every morning to run with me. Last night in fact, he slept in his car outside the house."

"He didn't!"

"Yes, he did. Didn't you let him change here this morning?"

"Well, yes I did."

"He's not planning to do so every night is he? For Heaven's sake the neighbors will talk."

"No, he is not. Last night is a onetime thing. He will however, be running with me in the mornings."

"Maggie, what does he want me to do?" asked Dr. Gordon.

"Just be aware of things around you."

He looked at Maggie and then Estelle. Finally he said, "Estelle, find me a blanket. I'm not leaving tonight."

"But the neighbors," Estelle protested.

"I don't give a fig about the neighbors. I do care you and Maggie are safe. Tonight I sleep on the sofa."

"It's not necessary. You may sleep in Martin's old room. I'll go make up the bed." Estelle left the room to get the bed ready.

"Thank you, Dr. Gordon," Maggie said.

"I think it's time you call me James or Jim, Maggie. Since I am going to marry your mother, it will be a bit awkward if you continue to call me Dr. Gordon."

"Ok, Jim, I will try."

Estelle returned to show Jim where the bedroom was and where he could find fresh linens in the morning. Maggie made her way to her room. Her mother would feel safe tonight. She hoped the Sheriff would have a plan soon.

Maggie met the Sheriff outside in the morning. They started off on their run. About halfway, he motioned to Maggie to stop.

"What's wrong?"

"Nothing, I think I have a way to trap Laura and I want to run it by you."

Maggie who'd been stretching stopped and looked directly at the Sheriff. "Go on."

"As I understand it, Ashton Margaret wants to meet her father and Laura has always forbidden it. What if she was contacted by Erika with a message her father would like to meet her? We could send her airline tickets and have Erika pick her up. We could arrange a meeting between Austin and his daughter."

"You think it would get Laura here?"

"It's worth a try. She would have to do something to keep the meeting from happening."

"Would Austin agree to this?"

"I think so. It would get him out from under Laura's thumb and we might get him to tell us all the things she's put him up to."

"Which would be good. I think you should try it."

"Okay, let's finish this run. I'll pull in Austin and put a call into Erika. Let's get the ball rolling."

They ran the rest of the way in silence. Back at Maggie's mother's house, Estelle was waiting for them on the back porch.

"Sheriff, I have a phone call for you."

"Thanks."

They both entered the house. Dr. Gordon was busy setting the table for four. Maggie headed for the shower. The Sheriff took the phone.

When Maggie finished her shower, she dressed and went to the kitchen. She was surprised to see the Sheriff had also showered and was dressed for the day.

"I want you all to know Austin Howard was picked up this morning and Erika Estwick will be in my office in half an hour. We are going to see if we can bring Laura Gilbert home to Timberview."

"Wonderful," Estelle said, "now maybe life can get back to normal."

"Mom, I think we still need to be taking precautions. I, for one, remember there were two voices in the school the first day. Austin Howard only accounts for one of them."

"I agree with Maggie," Dr. Gordon said, "We cannot stop being vigilant yet."

"Well, I suppose you are all right," Estelle conceded.

They ate breakfast in silence, everyone keeping their thoughts to themselves. After breakfast, Maggie and the Sheriff left. The Sheriff headed to his office and Maggie went on to the school.

Maggie visually checked the parking lot before exiting her car. She was starting to see shadows where there were none. She could see Amy Walsh and Hope had already arrived. She got out of her car and headed toward the school.

She found both Amy and Hope in the office. "Good morning," she said.

"Good morning, Maggie," the women said in unison then chuckled.

"Hope has Amy apprised you of our meeting last night?"

"No, she was waiting for you."

"Let's go into my office. Hope you can forward the phones in there."

Once in the office, Amy started, "I didn't want to alarm Hope so I waited for you."

"I appreciate it."

"Okay, I am here and I need to know what is going on."

Amy looked at Maggie and Maggie nodded.

"Hope, we think we know who is behind all of this. We are working on a plan to bring this person to Timberview so she can be brought to justice."

"It's a woman? And you are telling me, she is not even here?" Hope asked incredulously. "How is it possible?"

Maggie answered, "It has to do with something happened when I was in high school. It ended sometime when I was in college and has had twenty years to ferment. Austin Howard has been the pawn used to create all the problems, but he is only a small part of it."

"Maggie is giving you the short version," Amy said, "the part which affects you and everyone in the school is we will need to screen all of Maggie's calls and visitors."

"I already do."

"Yes, you do however; the woman we are looking for is Laura Gilbert and she will tell you, she is an old friend of Maggie's."

"Which doesn't mean she will get to see Maggie," Hope protested.

"The woman is ruthless. She will know things about you, you thought no one knew. She will use those things to make you give her access to Maggie."

"There is nothing for her to know about me."

"She has used Matt Mitchell's children."

"Two of my children are in this building. The other is in the middle school. Are you telling me they are not safe?"

"We don't know for sure. The oldest one needs to be aware of his surroundings and should never be anywhere alone."

"How am I supposed to tell him? He's already in class?"

"I have taken care of it. We sent your husband and an officer to talk to him."

"Thank you," Hope said relieved. "Now what do you want me to do?"

"We installed a tracker on your phone. If you should receive a call from this woman or any suspicious call, I want you to depress the button which starts the tracker. Otherwise, the same thing the Sheriff told people last night goes for you and your family, be aware of your surroundings and don't go anyplace alone."

"This is too easy. Are you sure you don't need me to do anything else?"

"No, just be yourself and we'll do the rest."

"I can be me."

"Good, guess we better open for the day. The staff will be arriving any minute. Maggie, you want to take the fourth and fifth grade wing this morning and I'll take the little ones?"

"Great idea, Amy, you can do the lower level and I'll do the upper."

"I'll get to it then." Amy left the office.

Hope returned to the front office and Maggie went to the fourth and fifth grade wing to welcome her staff to the new day. When she finished the upper floors it was time to greet the children. Maggie took her place at the front door and saw Amy Walsh was at the entrance to the upper grades.

The day was off to a normal start. Maggie did her second walkthrough changing ends with Amy. She had a feeling today would be a calm one, too bad she didn't feel calm.

The day proceeded without any incidents, but Maggie continued to have a nagging feeling something was not right. She talked with Hope about it at lunch time.

"Things seem almost too good today."

"I know," Hope replied, "no angry parents, no mix-ups on busses, nothing out of the ordinary. It's a nice change."

"Hope, I have this feeling something terrible is going to happen. I just cannot seem to shake it. I feel so silly thinking this way."

"Well, I can't say I blame you for thinking it. There has been nothing ordinary about the start to this school year."

"Maybe that's all it is, but I don't know," Maggie chuckled, "maybe I'm just getting paranoid."

"No, I think with all the things happening it's like we are always waiting for the next thing to happen."

"You could be right."

Maggie went on to supervise the cafeteria and then out onto the playground. All she could see anywhere were happy children. Maybe her fears were nothing after all.

At the end of the day, she did her walkthrough of the building. All of her staff was finishing up and making their way to their cars in twos and threes. Everyone was taking the advice of the Sheriff. Maggie hoped this would soon be a thing of the past. She returned to her office to close up and found both Hope and Amy waiting for her.

"The rule applies to everyone. I can't have Hope leaving alone and I can't have you leaving alone," Amy stated firmly.

"Give me just a minute," Maggie said as she went to her office to shut down her computer and turn off her tea pot.

The three of them left the building together. Maggie noted all three of their cars were parked together. Hope and Amy must have moved their cars during the day.

With cheerful good-byes each woman got into her car and headed for home. It had been a peaceful day. So, why did Maggie have this uneasy feeling?

Maggie continued to have her feeling of something about to happen all the way home. She pulled in the driveway and saw her mother's car was gone. She hoped it meant her mom was spending the evening with Dr. Gordon. Maggie was still having trouble calling him by his first name. Maybe she'd ask if she could call him Dr. G, the way she had referred to him as a teen. It was something to think about.

She went into the house. There was no note on the counter which was unusual, but everything seemed unusual these days. Maggie headed for her room, a shower and change of clothes. She might get the book she was reading finished tonight. She headed for the kitchen to see what she might throw together for a quick dinner. She found some fresh spinach and makings for a salad. She started fixing it while she tried to figure out what else she could have. That's when the phone rang.

Maggie picked up the phone and said, "Hello."

"Maggie Parsons?" asked the gruff voice on the other end.

"Yes it is."

"I have your mother."

"Excuse me?"

"You heard me, I have your mother."

Maggie took a deep breath trying to calm herself, "What do you want?"

"I want you to turn in your resignation by 9 am tomorrow morning. I want it effective immediately. Then you get the old lady back."

The person on the other end of the phone hung up. Maggie quickly dialed Dr. Gordon's number her heart pounding and a feeling of panic rising. He had an extension in his home and was known to make house calls after hours.

"Dr. Gordon."

"Thank goodness, this is Maggie Parsons, is my mom with you?"

"No, we didn't have any plans for tonight."

"Oh, no, oh no!"

"Maggie, calm down and tell me what's going on."

"Someone just called and said they had mom. They want me to resign by tomorrow morning. I have to call the police."

"You call. I'm on my way over."

Maggie disconnected the phone and dialed 9-1-1.

"9-1-1 dispatch how may I help you?"

"This is Maggie Parsons. My mom has been kidnapped."

"Okay, Mrs. Parsons, give me your address?"

Maggie quickly rattled off her mother's address.

"We'll have someone there in just a few minutes. Please stay on the line with me until the officers arrive," the dispatcher droned her usual comment then said, "What makes you think your mother was kidnapped?"

"I just had a phone call from her kidnappers," Maggie said with exasperation.

"What did they say?"

"They told me to resign from my job and I'd get her back."

"Do you hear the sirens?"

"Yes."

"Good stay with me just a few more minutes until the officers arrive."

"I'm waiting."

"Do you have a super sensitive job?"

"No, I'm the elementary principal," Maggie answered. "The officers are at the door. Thank you."

She hung up the phone and admitted the two officers.

"Officers Smith and Brown, Mrs. Parsons, can you tell us what is going on?"

"Come in gentlemen," Maggie said as she led the way to the living room. She motioned for the men to have a seat on the sofa and sat in her father's chair. Once everyone was seated she continued, "I received a call saying someone had my mother and the only way I can get her back is to resign by tomorrow morning." Maggie got to her feet and started pacing.

"You are sure your mother is missing?"

"Her car is not here and I called Dr. Gordon, he said they did not have plans tonight."

"Is there any place else she might have gone?"

"I didn't think to call my brother," Maggie said, "oh goodness I should." She stood to walk to the phone.

Officer Brown stopped her, "Wait before you call him. We need to ask you some more questions."

Maggie sat back down. At that point, Dr. Gordon came through the back door.

"Maggie, Maggie where are you?"

"In the living room, Dr. G," she answered him.

He entered the living room and went to Maggie's side. "Is there any word?"

"No, these officers were just asking if there was any place else Mom could have gone," she looked at him and said, "I forgot to call Marty."

"I will call for you."

He went for the phone and the officers did not stop him. They turned back to Maggie, "Who did this caller say he was?"

"He didn't. His voice was tinny sounding, as though he was trying to disguise it."

"Then you didn't recognize him?"

"No, I'm afraid not. Shouldn't you be doing something?" she asked her voice trembling with the fear she felt.

Dr. Gordon hung up the phone and turned to the two officers and Maggie, "There seems to have been a mistake. Estelle is at her son's visiting. She was about to call Maggie and tell her, she'd be staying there for dinner. Maggie, she said there was a note on the counter."

Maggie stood there stunned, and then sank into her father's chair. Her mother was at Marty's. She hadn't been kidnapped. Someone was really trying to discredit her.

Officer Smith rose and said, "Well, I guess we won't be needed here."

"Thank you, Officers," Dr. Gordon said leading them to the back door. "I'll take care of Maggie; she's been under a strain lately."

"She shouldn't be calling in false reports."

"No and we'll make sure she doesn't do it again. Thank you."

The two men left and Dr. Gordon went back to the living room. Maggie was still sitting in her father's chair. She looked so frightened.

"Maggie, do you want something?"

She looked up tears were running down her face, "Dr. Gordon, who hates me so much that they want me to look like I'm losing my mind? I cannot believe that Laura Gilbert can be behind something like this."

"I don't know but I do know the Sheriff is working on it."

"I can't keep putting people in danger. Maybe I should turn in my resignation."

"Which means you're willing to let the bad guys win. Are you sure it's what you want? No, don't answer. Think long and hard before you make a decision."

"Ok," she said tearfully.

There was a knock on the back door. Dr. Gordon went to answer it. Sheriff Norton was standing there. Dr. Gordon invited him in, "She's pretty shook up and is thinking of resigning. Maybe you can talk some sense into her."

"I'll try. Where is she?"

"Living room, I'll clean up the kitchen. Don't think she's eaten."

"I'll see she eats."

"Then I'll let myself out the back door when I'm done."

"Thanks, Doc."

Maggie was curled up in her father's chair when the Sheriff walked into the living room. She stood when she saw him.

"I'm so sorry. I didn't mean to waste anybody's time."

"You didn't. Someone is trying to get to you. We must be getting close."

"You think so?" she asked hopefully.

"I think we need to take you to get something to eat. Then we will figure out just what happened."

Maggie agreed and they locked up the house and left in the Sheriff's truck.

"Where are we going for dinner?" she asked absently.

"I thought I'd surprise you. I hope you like Chinese."

"I do."

"Good. This is one of my favorite places."

They drove in silence for about twenty minutes. They pulled up in front of a store front restaurant in Ridgeway. The inside of the restaurant was elegantly furnished in ornate Chinese, rich reds and dark woods. Maggie couldn't help but look around the beautiful surroundings.

"How did you find this place?"

"I spend my time scouting out the best restaurants. I never know when I might want to whisk a beautiful lady to someplace secluded," he said smiling.

"Yeah, right, I've heard *that* before."

They looked at the menu and ordered their dinner and some white wine. Terry had ordered egg rolls and Maggie had ordered crab rangoons for appetizers. Those arrived and they shared. It was pleasant. When dinner arrived they each sampled some of the others. Maggie had moo goo gai pan and Terry had sweet and sour pork. Both had opted for fried rice. As they ate they talked about the phone call Maggie had received.

"It was a tinny sounding voice. I couldn't be sure whether it was a man or a woman."

"What made you think that someone could have your mom?"

"She always leaves a note and there wasn't one. I thought I was doing the right thing."

"You did."

"I just felt so foolish when Dr. Gordon told everyone that Mom was at Marty's."

"It's okay to make a mistake. Given that you had been told that someone had taken her, you did the right thing. Now I want to tell you the other thing that happened today."

Maggie looked at him hoping there was some good news. She was rewarded when he smiled and launched into the days accomplishments.

"Erika called Ashton-Margaret early this morning and issued an invitation to her to come and meet her father."

"What did she say?"

"Erika arranged for her to fly in tomorrow."

"Do you think it's why someone wanted me to resign by tomorrow?"

"It could very well be."

"So, when is Ashton-Margaret arriving? Does Aussie know yet?"

Terry smiled at Maggie, "She is arriving at three o'clock in the afternoon. Erika will be meeting her. Austin has been rounded up by one of my officers and put up in the local hotel. He will be there for the night. We arranged for him to get a haircut and a new suit. He'll be joining me at my office for the meeting."

"Why your office?"

"We thought it would be safer for Austin. Laura has been holding Ashton-Margaret over his head for nineteen years. We didn't want to take a chance she would try something."

"I thought the idea was to catch her trying something."

"It is the idea, but we really want to come through for Austin and get him on our side. Allowing him to actually meet with his daughter is our way of getting it done."

"Then take her to him at the hotel. Don't make her meet her Dad in a police station."

"I cannot control the hotel. I can control the station. I'm going to let them meet in my office. I won't be inside; I'll be outside making sure they have all the time they need."

"Okay, but how do you plan to get Laura to town?"

"I think she's close now. I believe she was behind your phone call."

"I don't get it. Why?"

"She wanted you to doubt yourself. If you doubt yourself, you won't take the precautions I asked you to take. You'll give into her and resign instead of showing her you've got what it takes. You start to wonder if you are crazy."

"Well you've got the crazy part right. This is the second time Officers Smith and Brown have been called by me and it's turned into nothing."

"They did just what they were supposed to. They answered your call and took the information you had."

"But once again it seems as though I was crying wolf."

"Exactly what someone wants you to think. All of my staff know what is going on. Which is why they were keeping you focused trying to get all the information you had."

"They did a great job. I didn't feel foolish until Doc Gordon said Mom was safe at Marty's."

"Well, enough. Let's get you home. Your mom should be there by now and we don't want her to worry."

"Thank you. This was wonderful."

He smiled at Maggie and handed her a fortune cookie. She took it and opened it immediately.

"Oh, look," she cried, "it says good fortune is mine."

"Mine says I am destined to spend more time with a beautiful lady." He smiled at Maggie. She blushed. They left the restaurant and headed for home.

At the back door he said good-night and made sure she was inside then he parked down the street where he had a clear view of the house and settled in. He wasn't there ten minutes when Mrs. Mills left the house. She was coming in his direction. He got out of his truck to see what was wrong.

"Mrs. Mills, I thought you were told not to go any place alone."

"I'm not alone; I'm standing here with you."

"What's the problem? Is Maggie okay?"

"Yes, she is okay. The problem is the neighbors are going to start talking. If you insist on guarding my daughter, you might as well be comfortable. Park your truck in the driveway and I've put blankets on the sofa."

"Yes, ma'am," was all he said, and then he added, "Why don't you ride back with me."

She nodded and took a seat in passenger side of the truck. He drove into her drive. They both got out and entered the house.

Maggie who watched the entire episode from the window was laughing when they entered.

"Margaret, do show some decorum," her mother said.

"Yes, Mom," she said as she stifled her laughter behind her hand.

Terry thought it was the most magical sound he'd ever heard.

Maggie handed him a pillow while Estelle got a sheet and the blankets. He made up the sofa as a bed and told the ladies he'd try not to snore too loudly.

Estelle gave a harrumph and went off to her room. Maggie made sure the Sheriff would be comfortable and then went to her room.

He could hear her giggling as he removed his shirt and belt. It was a sound he wanted to hear more often. Tonight he would settle for knowing she was safe.

Maggie woke early and dressed in her running outfit and headed out to wake the Sheriff. She was surprised to see the blankets folded and the Sheriff already up. He was holding a cup of coffee and was dressed to run.

"Good morning, Sunshine, ready to run?"

"I am."

"Then let's be off."

They headed out the back door making sure it was locked. They took a different route this morning and were back in twenty minutes.

Estelle was in the kitchen. She looked up when they entered and asked, "Who has been cooking in my kitchen?" she asked arching her brow.

The Sheriff smiled sheepishly and said, "I was, did you find breakfast in the oven?"

"I saw something was there but didn't want to disturb it in case it was a surprise."

"No, just my way of saying thank you for letting me sleep on the couch. My truck is not the most comfortable place to sleep."

"Well, you two get cleaned up and I'll get the table set since I don't have to cook."

Maggie went to one bathroom and the Sheriff went to the other. Both emerged a few minutes later showered and dressed for the day.

Estelle had the table set. The Sheriff went to the oven and took out the quiche he'd made. He brought it to the table and placed it on a hot pad.

"I hope you like it. I wasn't sure what you liked."

"So, what did you find to put in it?" Estelle asked.

"I found some bacon, sausage, tomato, onion, and some cheese."

"Sounds delicious," Maggie said enthusiastically, "are you serving?"

"I am," he said and started serving the quiche.

Breakfast was over quickly. Both Maggie and the Sheriff had jobs to go to. Estelle found herself cleaning up after breakfast, but she didn't mind. It had been nice to have someone else cook for a change.

The day was normal for Maggie. She took a couple phone calls from parents, wrote her weekly reports and sent them to Mr. Whitehead. Then she had time to spend with the children at lunch. First graders had a story they were learning so she went to hear them read.

The Sheriff called her at three fifteen to let her know Ashton-Margaret had arrived and was on her way to the police station. He'd keep her up to date as things happened.

She stood at the fourth and fifth grade wing as the children left for home. She watched the children give hugs to Amy Walsh as if she really were the assistant principal. Maggie would be sorry to see her go when this was all over.

She did her end of the day walk through with Amy at her side. Amy stayed back as Maggie spoke to her staff. They ended up in the office. Hope was ready. Maggie grabbed her purse and the three women walked to their cars together.

Hope said to Maggie, "Remember to give me a call if you need help moving."

"I will. I really think I have it covered, though."

"Have a good week-end, Maggie."

"You both have good week-ends."

They got in their cars and drove to their separate homes.

Estelle was in the kitchen when Maggie came through the back door.

"Maggie, Martin tells me you are moving this week-end. Do you think its wise?"

"I'm getting furniture in the house, Mom. I probably won't be spending the night there before Sunday."

"I'm just concerned. Laura is still out there. She's already made a nuisance out of herself. I don't want you getting hurt."

"If the Sheriff's plan works, they hope to have her in custody tonight."

"Which would be a relief."

"Yes, it would. Then maybe I could have a normal job with normal problems." She walked out of the kitchen and toward her bedroom. She just wanted a quiet evening with her mother. She was not up to a fight. She changed into jeans and a t-shirt and headed back toward the kitchen.

"Oh, Maggie, I forgot to tell you. Jim wants to take us both to dinner tonight."

"No problem. Did he say where he was taking us?"

"He found some Chinese place in Ridgeway."

Maggie started to laugh.

Estelle looked at her daughter and said, "Just what is so funny?"

When she finally caught her breath Maggie answered, "The Sheriff took me there last night while you were with Marty and his family."

"I see," Estelle said. "It would seem your Sheriff and my intended are trying to keep us both safe."

"So it would seem. I'll go change my shirt." Maggie left to change just as Dr. Gordon knocked on the back door.

"Did the Sheriff tell you he'd taken Maggie to this restaurant last night?" Estelle demanded as he came through the door.

"He mentioned it. I asked him if he knew of a good place to eat that was out of town."

"Really, you two are taking this cloak and dagger stuff too seriously."

"No, we're not. They have a direct link between Laura Gilbert and the death of Maggie's family," he said softly.

Estelle gasped. "I don't believe it."

"Evidently aside from Austin's testimony there is some other evidence. They are hoping to have her in custody soon. All of the patrol cars have her photo and are on the lookout for her."

"I suppose it means I'll have the Sheriff sleeping on my sofa again tonight," she said resignedly.

"It's for the best. I like the idea he's keeping my two best girls safe." He gave Estelle a hug and looked up as Maggie entered the room.

"I'm sorry I didn't mean to interrupt."

"You didn't, but if everyone is ready we have dinner reservations."

They drove to Ridgeway discussing the advertisement Dr. Gordon had run for a new town doctor. He had put the person needed to be willing to make after hours house calls and be available for grocery store diagnoses.

Which brought a laugh from everyone. There was much discussion as to whether or not they'd be able to find a doctor willing to take on the whole town. There weren't many country doctors left, they were a dying breed.

Dinner was spectacular. They each had an appetizer. They also shared dinners. Dr. Gordon had ordered sweet and sour chicken, her mother had mu shu pork, and Maggie stayed with the moo goo gai pan she'd had the night before. They all had fried rice. They had Chinese tea with their meal and fortune cookies for dessert. They were full and heading home when Maggie's cell phone rang.

"Hello."

"Maggie, it's Terry Norton."

"Hi, what's up?"

"I need to know where you are."

"We just left the restaurant in Ridgeway. We are about twenty minutes from home. Why?"

"No reason, I just want to know when I need to be at the house."

"Seriously tell me what's going on."

"I'll tell all of you when I see you. I'll be at the house when you get there."

"Okay, see you soon." Maggie hung up her phone and said, "The Sheriff will be waiting for us at the house. He has something to tell us."

"I for one hope it's good news," said Estelle.

"I agree with the idea of good news," echoed Dr. Gordon.

"I guess we'll all know soon."

They drove the rest of the way in silence.

The Sheriff was sitting in his truck in front of the house when Dr. Gordon pulled in. He was out of his truck and heading for the house before they had a chance to get out. He opened the door for Maggie and pulled her close to him. Dr. Gordon came quickly around the car to assist Estelle. He had picked up the caution in the Sheriff's movements. Quickly leading Estelle to the back door he stood behind her as she opened the door. Once inside, the Sheriff locked the door and sent everyone to the living room. He said, "Only turn on the dimmest light and stay away from the windows."

In the living room Estelle turned on a small reading lamp. Dr. Gordon pulled the drapes across the window so no one would be able to see in. Then he joined Estelle on the sofa. Maggie gravitated to her father's chair, wondering what had happened to cause all this covert activity.

The Sheriff entered the room and took a seat in the straight back chair. "I have some very serious information to give you. I also have a plan."

"Well, spit it out, young man," Estelle said tersely. "I don't like this kind of behavior."

"I'm sorry, Mrs. Mills. I wanted you to be safe."

"I suppose," she conceded, "What is this information?"

"Laura Gilbert showed up in town this late this afternoon. She was raving like a mad woman at Glen's store. Then she went to Matt's hardware and was ranting there. She went from there to the Blake's. She threatened to take Ashton's children from her. Finally, she ended up at Austin Howard's house. She broke in and destroyed everything she could. My officers were behind her but, she slipped away. She's not been here or to Marty's as far as I know. I expect her to wait until late to try something. Mrs. Mills," he said turning directly to Estelle, "I don't want to put your sensibilities to a test, but I want you to go home with Dr. Gordon tonight. I already have officers in the area so you will be safe."

"I will not be driven from my home!"

"It's not a request. I don't want you here. Laura is after Maggie and I don't want you caught in the crossfire. Please go pack an overnight bag, we don't have much time."

"Where is Maggie going to stay?"

"Here, she is the bait."

Maggie stifled a gasp. Her mother looked horrified.

"Stell, the Sheriff knows what he is doing. Maggie will be safe," Dr. Gordon said in his quiet voice.

Reluctantly Estelle went to her room; she left the hall light on and packed a few things she'd need for an overnight stay. She turned off the hall light and returned to the living room. Maggie was standing between Dr. Gordon and the Sheriff. She quietly stepped forward and hugged her mother. As she did she whispered, "I'll be okay. See you tomorrow. I love you."

Estelle just nodded and hugged Maggie tighter. Then she let go and walked to Dr. Gordon.

"I'm ready," she looked at the Sheriff and said, "You will call me in the morning." It was not a question.

"I'll keep Maggie safe and have her call you in the morning."

After the two of them left, the Sheriff turned to Maggie, "I'm sorry for all of this. I need you to lock the door when I leave. I took the spare key before you got here. I'm going to park my truck a couple blocks away and walk back. Don't leave the porch light on I don't want to be seen."

"What if she gets here before you get back?'

"I have two unmarked cars parked in driveways where they can see the house. She won't get in. Remember I have the key."

"I cannot sit here in the dark."

"I don't want you to. Turn on whatever lights you would have on if you were waiting for your mom to come home."

"Okay."

"One more thing, in case Laura is watching, I want you to kiss me goodnight. I want her convinced I am not coming back."

"I can make her believe."

"Okay, then if you are ready, it's time for me to leave."

He opened the back door and Maggie followed him onto the porch. He turned and took her in his arms. They kissed goodnight and he waited for her to go back inside before heading to his truck.

Maggie locked the door and leaned against it. She had been affected by the kiss. She had not kissed a man since she married Ben. She felt herself going weak in the knees with Terry's kiss. She could not become involved with the Sheriff. It was way too soon. She shoved off from the door, put the light on over the stove, and put the kettle on to boil. Then she walked into the living room, turned on the light next to her father's chair, and found the book she'd been trying to read all summer. It would keep her mind busy while she waited for the Sheriff to return. She settled into the chair and read while she waited for the water to boil.

When she heard the tea kettle whistle, she put down her book and went into the kitchen, and began making her tea. All of the sudden the lights went out. She heard glass breaking in the bedroom area of the house. Maggie remained rooted to the where she was; not knowing what to expect next.

As her eyes grew accustomed to the dark she saw a figure coming from the living room.

"Stop right there," she called.

"Why, Maggie, that's no way to greet and old friend."

Maggie recognized Laura's voice and replied, "Old friends don't break in, and they don't kill someone else's family."

"Oh, well, it was just business."

"It wasn't just business to me. It was my husband and my children. Whatever did I do to you?"

"You and the high and mighty Ashton deserted me when I needed you most. Why, because Austin was my baby's father? Were you so sure he'd still want you if I had his baby?"

"Laura, we didn't know. Our mothers didn't tell us. In fact, I only found out a couple of weeks ago."

"Yeah, right," Maggie could hear the bitterness in Laura's voice, "I suppose it's why they kept sending me money;

anything to keep me away from their precious daughters. My father had a heart attack. He couldn't live with the shame."

"I'm sorry about your father."

"I suppose you're going to tell me you didn't know about him either. Why should I believe you? You kept on going with your life. You married Mr. Right and had twins. Your life was perfect."

"We were happy. You took all it from me. Isn't it enough revenge?"

"Did you know I named her for my two best friends? Then I kept her as far from here as I possibly could, until now."

"You could have tried to call me. Even later you could have tried. Tell me why you would want to hurt Matt and Glen?"

"Right, like you would want to hear my sad story," She moved into the kitchen.

Maggie saw the glint of metal in her hand. "I would like to hear your story. I'd like to know why you think you have to hurt us all. We were friends."

"Some friends," Laura sneered. "First you shut out Aussie like he'd committed a crime. I tried to get you to forgive him."

"I remember, I just didn't know why?"

"Because I loved him," Laura wailed. "All you could see was he lied and had to be punished. We had to sneak around to see each other."

"You didn't," Maggie started.

"You would have cut me out, too. He even came to the college every week-end to see me. Even then all he could talk about was you. I shared your letters with him. We wrote back to you and you never even had a clue."

"I loved your letters. You always sounded so happy."

"I was in love with a man who loved another woman. When I got pregnant, I hoped he'd look at me differently. Do you know what he said??"

"I have no idea."

"He said, 'I'd be happy to settle down if Maggie was having my child."

"Oh, Laura, I'm so sorry."

"I'll bet you are," Laura said acidly.

"So, you break into my mother's home and threaten me? Is this your big plan?"

"No, I fully intend for you to commit suicide tonight."

"I'm not going to kill myself. I have no reason to do so."

"You are distraught about the deaths of your family and the terrible things which have plagued the school because of you. You regret all the bad things you did to Aussie and I and it was too much for you, so you decided to end it."

"You are wrong."

"What you don't have any regrets?"

"It's not what I meant," Maggie replied stalling for time and hoping the Sheriff would hurry. "I have regrets, but they don't have to do with the school or you and Austin."

"Which figures as always you are only concerned for yourself," Laura hissed and started to raise the gun.

At that moment as Laura raised the gun, the back door opened and the Sheriff stepped in. Laura was distracted and Maggie threw her cup of hot water in Laura's face. Laura screamed and dropped the gun. Maggie tackled her and knocked her to the floor at the same time screaming, "Bring your handcuffs!"

The Sheriff not thinking twice came to Maggie's rescue with his handcuffs in his hand. The back door burst open and two undercover officers with large flashlights took in the scene.

"Sheriff, you okay?"

"Yes, but we need a bus, we have burns." He turned to Laura Gilbert and began reading her, her rights, "Laura Gilbert, you are under arrest. You have the right to remain silent. Anything you say can and will be used against you in a court of law. You have the right to an attorney. If you cannot afford one, one will be appointed for you. Do you understand these rights as I have read them to you?"

Laura nodded. She stood mute while they took her to the ambulance and checked her out. Her burns were treated and she was taken to the police station for booking.

The Sheriff walked back into the house carrying a large flashlight. "Maggie," he called. "Where are you?"

"I'm in the living room."

"I'm coming in." He followed the glow of his flashlight and saw that Maggie had started a fire in the fireplace and lit some candles. She was huddled in her father's chair.

He went over and took her in his arms. "It's over."

"Not really, I have to figure out how to explain to Mom we have no power and there is a broken window in Marty's old room," she chuckled nervously.

The Sheriff released her and said, "I've already got someone coming to check on the power. I'll have the window taken care of tomorrow. Tonight I'll get a piece of plywood out of my truck and cover the window. Are you going to be okay here while I go get my truck or do you want to take a midnight stroll?"

"I think I'd like the stroll."

Okay, get a jacket. I'll put the candles out and bank the fire."

Maggie went to get a jacket and returned to the living room. Terry stood there with his flashlight on. He radioed he needed a car here so the house wasn't further broken into. Then the two of them set off walking to get his truck.

When they returned, they found officers in a patrol car in front of the house had been there when power was restored to the house. They took the plywood out of the Sheriff's truck and put it over the broken window. Maggie thanked them both and sent them home.

"Sorry, Maggie, but you are stuck with me tonight. I'm sure Laura is locked up and will stay that way, but I promised your mother I would keep you safe."

"She left blankets on the sofa just in case. I'll find the pillows."

He set the kettle on again and Maggie went to find pillows. He brought two cups of tea into the living room. Maggie was checking on the fire.

"Come sit by me and drink some tea," he said.

"Is it spiked with something?" Maggie asked suspiciously.

"Just milk, but I can find something else if you'd like."

She laughed and came over to sit next to him. After sipping her tea she said, "At least I now understand what made her think I was the problem."

"It seems even though he was dating her, all Austin could talk about was you. It wasn't until she got pregnant, she figured out he was using her in the hopes of getting back together with you."

"So, all these years she has blamed me for everything wrong in her life?"

"Essentially, yes. Then she found ways she could use her daughter to get Austin to do what she wanted. He was driving the semi that hit your family. He really went into the bottle after the accident. He did not know the kids were in the car. Which is how he lost his job. Even after that, Laura still kept their daughter from him."

"He thinks I stole his happiness because he couldn't see his daughter?"

"He's been pretty messed up for a long time."

"What will happen to him?"

"He's going to turn state's witness against Laura. He will get immunity from prosecution. Laura on the other hand will be spending the rest of her life in jail."

"He will get to spend time with his daughter then?"

"He will be on probation, have to do some community service, and must get help for his alcohol problem. Ashton-Margaret is hoping to move here when she is done with school. It seems she's studying to be an art teacher. She'll be looking for a job."

"Let's hope we can help her find one. I think I'm ready to sleep now."

"Okay, I'll see you in the morning." He picked up their cups and headed toward the kitchen.

Maggie went into her bedroom, changed into her pajamas, and crawled into bed. She was asleep before her head hit the pillow. She slept a deep and dreamless sleep for the first time since the accident.

The next morning Maggie and the Sheriff went for a run. When they returned home, Maggie called Dr. Gordon's and spoke to her mother. She told her, Laura had broken in last night and the Sheriff had arrested her. He was also having the window replaced. Maggie reminded her mother, she, Marty and the Sheriff were going to move Maggie's furniture to her new house.

"You'll be home tonight?" Estelle asked.

"Yes, I'm not sure what time though."

"Well, I thought we'd grill outside. I'll call and arrange for Marty's family to join us. You ask Sheriff Norton if he'd like to come."

"Sure, it sounds like fun."

Maggie and the Sheriff left for Marty's and then went on to Davenport to load the trucks. Maggie was truly ready to start a new chapter in her life. Her old one was officially over. The new one held all sorts of promises.

# ACKNOWLEDGMENTS

First I'd like to thank my editors who have worked tirelessly to fix all my mistakes. Jamie Kline, my daughter, and Donavee Vigus, my mom, both of whom are avid readers, working women, and busy homemakers. Their requests for the next chapter kept me going.

An extra thank you goes to Jamie as she edited twice. Once after the first writing and again after it was restored following the crash of my computer.

Also I'd like to give a special thank you to my readers, many of whom are my biggest cheering section. I hope you will enjoy this book as much as you have enjoyed my others.

# ABOUT THE AUTHOR

Photo credit: Holly Denstedt Photography

Retired teacher Rebecka Vigus spends her time writing, reading, crocheting, hiking, and swimming. She travels seeking the ideal place to call home. Ms. Vigus has been writing since she was in her pre-teens. Her first book was poetry, *Only a Start and Beyond*. Since then she has penned five, full-length novels, one book for children, several short stories, and even a self-help book for tweens and teens. Ms. Vigus has been listed as a Michigan Author and Illustrator at the State of Michigan website.

www.ingramcontent.com/pod-product-compliance
Lightning Source LLC
Chambersburg PA
CBHW050616190726
48283CB00007B/2445